I0684678

Avesta Eeschatology Compared with the Books of Daniel and Revelations

Lawrence Heyworth Mills

Contents

AVESTA EESCHATOLOGY COMPARED WITH THE

BOOKS OF DANIEL AND REVELATIONS

BY

Lawrence Heyworth Mills

CHAPTER I.

THE CASE PRIMA FACIE.

Literary and Historical Connection Between the Avesta and the Exilic Semitic Scriptures.

THE supposed Zoroastrian elements in the Book of Daniel have always been considered to be very striking; but as they form a part of a whole with their predecessors and successors, they cannot be estimated altogether aside from other Exilic matter. So that the entire ancient religious literature of the Jews is brought into the question, though as a matter of course the limits of the space at my disposal here do not permit me to treat the whole of it in this section. And if Zoroastrian elements appear anywhere at all within the Jewish ancient literature, we may take it for granted that the entire mass of Zoroastrian doctrine must have exerted the most decided influence upon the developments of Jewish Exilic and of the Christian theology, for a part here proves the presence and in-fluence of the whole.

And this at once, as I need not say, entails the gravest possible consequences in our decisions as to the vital matter of precedence or sequence in the intellectual forces here brought into consideration, as they develop themselves and become manifest in our histories of religious thought.

The objective before us, then, is to illustrate, from various points of view taken here and for the present necessarily from restricted portions of the Semitic Scriptures, the admitted fact that the Jewish tribes entered a new intellectual world at the so-called Captivity, and then that this sphere was largely dominated by Medo-Persian as well as by Babylonian ideas, and that it was therefore to a degree Zoroastrian, and that upon this it was built up as a mass of national religious sentiment and system

It is, however, necessary for me to interpose here an important precautionary salvo. It is this: that the Per-sian theology with which we are here called upon to deal, is, if we must judge from its surviving documents, divisible into two branches or schools: the Median, the more thoroughly Zoroastrian as represented by the Ze-nd-Avesta, and the Southern school of Persepolis as repre-sented by the Achæmenian Inscriptions. It is of course possible that these two portions of the Mazda-worship interest may not really have differed from each other as much as their now surviving documents would seem to indicate; while their close relation in spite of all conceivable divergence is not for a moment to be contested, for they have much that is essential in common; and they must each be considered as at times express-ing but one and the same phase of religious conception; but still it is safer to form our judgments from these actually surviving writings, particularly as each of them is of a signal character in its particular sphere.

So looked upon, it is chiefly the Median Mazda worship, that is to say, the Zoroastrian, centering in Ragha, which is here brought into bearing with the grave questions which we are discussing, rather than the Achæmenian or Daric inscriptional elements on which I here chiefly rely, and to which I here first of all refer as at once. With the two lores in view, that is to say, with that of the Exilic Pharisaism on the one side and that of the Zend-Avesta on the other, we have two occurrences of the most important possible of religious ideas that have ever been propagated, present in two religious systems brought closely into connection with each other, as I show just below, one of which, the Jewish Exilic, dominates all Western civilization; and this actual historical literary connection between them, if it be proved to our satisfaction to be a fact, cannot help but afford occasion for the deepest possible reflection and inquiry, which must also be regarded as pre-eminently interesting from several points of view.

We must first of all mention and make clear what may be called the incontestable points of literary connection between these Iranian and Semitic lores from this line of thought, corroborative particulars from other sources following in due course; for, as I have said, if anything at all approaching to a literary connection between the two centers of intelligence can be established, our case is by the very fact of it made out, with all that it involves; for Zoroastrianism is the main document of our eschatology, a fact which should be taken everywhere for granted, as the slightest examination would confirm it.[1] And first of all in our further procedure we have to note the general features of the situation.

　* * *

The entire mass of the Medo-Persian Mazda-worship is, as we assert, brought into close association with Judaism in an unparalleled manner in the familiar passages which meet us in Chronicles, Ezra, Nehemiah, the later Isaiah, Daniel, etc., and in the entire Exilic and post-Exilic Jewish and Christian literatures, that is to say, when this mass of profoundly interesting religious detail is studied

> [1] From start to finish we have everywhere in Zoroastrianism the main points of our eschatology; there was no other lore at the period of the oldest Avesta which so expressed the doctrines almost in modern terms.

in connection with the Achæmenian inscriptions of the Persian kings whose edicts are cited in the Bible. To speak of Exilic Jewish history is then to speak of Persian history in one of its most interesting episodes, and vice versa; for such allusions center in the superlative circumstances, of the so-called Return of the Jewish Tribes and the re-establishment of their religion upon its original representative site with the to us so momentous consequences. And no statements could be stronger, as might be said, than those well-known familiar ones which are every-where so prominent in the documents themselves, with perhaps Isaiah xliv or xlv at their head. The Persian Emperor who represented his religion (see the inscriptions) is there accepted as the "anointed of Yahveh"—an expression which carried with it the assurance of the existence of the deepest possible religious sentiment with regard to the exalted personage to whom it alludes; and this with a salvo in verse 7 which doubly accentuates the affirmatives. So much for the connection ***prima*** *facie.* But when we have said this we must proceed to mention here, although still only in a preliminary sense, some individual particulars, as a further succinct but necessary introduction of our subject, though some of these will necessarily occupy our attention again in their detail further on.

The first of them would be perhaps that truly monumental circumstance in the Medo-Persian Jewish religious history, the presence of the "Seven Spirits" of the Zend-Avesta in Job, Zechariah, Tobit and the Apocalypse. The first mentioned, the occurrence in Job, indeed lacks the mention of the number "Seven," but the "walking to and fro in the Earth" is characteristic, while in the occurrence in Tobit xii. 15 we have both the words together, and the ideas are especially clinched to the Iranian work by the mention of one of the oldest of the Gathic demons (Tobit iii. 8. 17; viii. 3) in close association with them (the seven Ameshaspends), added to which we have the Avesta city Ragha mentioned more than once, and all in the same book.

The tale of the Book of Tobit seems indeed to be a story largely centering about the Zoroastrian capital, if we might so call the most prominent place mentioned in the Avesta: see Tobit i. 10, 14: "And I went into Media and kept ten talents of silver in trust with Gabriel the brother of Gabrias at Rases, a city in Media" see also Tobit iv. I; iv. 20; v. 5; vi, 9; vi. 12; ix. 2; xiv. 4.

Ragha, as we know, was so completely Zoroastrian that the very name "Zarathushtra" became a civic title there of high order, and it was even used in the superlative degree as "most Zarathushtra," totally losing the significance of its original application to the particular family of the distinguished prophet.

Kohut[2] also with much probability likewise found the common Persian word Khshathra, which is also the name of the third Avestic Ameshaspend, in Esther as well as in Daniel. This would of course only help to illustrate still more the close Persian relation, which we may regard as hardly contested; but with much sagacity he noticed the "uer" of Ahasuerus, which equals "ver"; and in it he with much plausibility saw not only the Persian Khshathra—the "Ahas" having resulted, as so often in similar cases, from contraction plus the added incipient "A"— but he saw the Avestic Khshathra-vairya, the "ver" representing this latter part of the compositum, as indeed it does also in the Pahlavi middle Persian, Khshathra and Vairya also occurring in close association even in the Gathas. The asserted analogies between the Persian, the Jewish, and the Babylonian month-names, are also

[2] See his work cited below, now of course antiquated, but still suggestive. If indeed this recognition be not beyond dispute, it yet awakens our attention and our zeal to search for other analogies.

particularly significant. Not pausing upon what may be considered especially controversial in Benfey's attempted identifications here (see also his successors), it will be convenient to call especial attention to the signal word "Adar" (Atar), which is purely Persian, both in its literal meaning and in its here so significant application. No scholar can have failed to become aware that the word for fire, while well-nigh the most common word of its kind in the Persian, is at the same time perhaps the most sacred of its sort in that language; for the element was personified as an Angel and has a Yasht really, though not formally, devoted to it, and this in the genuine if yet later Avesta.

Zoroastrians have also been for a long time called "Fire worshipers," on account of their especial use of fire in worship, which was rather more pronounced than its adoption among the Hebrews except perhaps in the Exilic and post-Exilic times; and even here the use of the Seven Lamps to symbolize the Seven Spirits, which lingers in the Church is perhaps not so striking as the fire altars perpetually burning in the Zoroastrian temples. And the influence of the ideas which center in this "element" was so marked that an important province to the southwest of the Caspian Sea was named Azerbaigan Adharbagan.[3]

It was also in connection with the names of others of the most holy concepts in Iranian thought that the word "Adar" was so prominently adopted as the name of a Parsi month,[4] as it is also in both the Jewish and the As-syrian; and this circumstance, though it is not at all the most incisive of the initial features, is yet one of the most convincing, and affords formidable proof of early Iranian influence upon Babylon.

> [3] The Holy Fire was not perhaps as yet personified in the Gatha, but it is still most reverently mentioned. Some Parsis have, I think, cherished the belief that the fires upon the chief altars in the Fire Temples were originally supernaturally imparted.
>
> [4]As *adar* = "fire" was a word otherwise totally unknown to the Semitic languages in this sense, the facts are peculiarly important

As this item is so incisive in the impression which it makes upon us I will dwell for a moment longer upon it here.

Here is a month named "Adar" in the Babylonian, the Jewish and the Persian languages. To the Babylonian and the Hebrew, the term is wholly foreign, certainly so if it meant "fire" in Babylonian and Hebrew; but in the Iranian Medo-Persian it is one of the most common of all household terms, also emphatically sanctified for the sacrifice, and its application in Iranian to the naming of a month accentuates its distinction. To which then of the three languages, which each used it for a month, was it originally so applied?

Is it likely that the Babylonians developed out of their own speech, and as if by accident, a word which was externally identical with this Persian term, at once so common and so distinguished, and without the smallest hint from Persian usage applied it also to a month as the Iranians have done—a month being presumably as sacred an interval of time to the Babylonians as it was to the Iranians?[5]

Was it there used as a pure Syrian word "Adar" in a territory which may have been overrun by Persian influences at some immemorial epoch, (which is one of my present contentions), and which was at an early date soon after the first Exile actually known to have been so overrun, proving that this Iranian word may well have later crept into the earlier Hebrew texts in the ever-repeated recopying of manuscripts? Is it likely then that this term, universally used in Iranian for "fire," should have any other meaning when applied to a Syrian Deity, "fire" having universal claims to worship, an element which could not help, as we might almost say of it, be-

[5] See the word applied to a Syrian god in Palestine as reported not very long ago.

coming a god ? And if the Syrian, Assyrian, or Babylonian word meant "fire" also, its Iranian origin is certain. See also Tebeth, an Iranian word, which is also a Semitic month name, from Avesta, *tap,* "to burn," cp. Tabistan = "summer." Not to speak of Ab as again a month of "water," nor of Tishri as Tishtrya, Tishtar, being a prominent Persian star and later ***Sirius, yet also with the others applied to a Persian month;*** see even Khisleu which might easily recall Khashathra as contracted, a Parsi month, as "s"="t," "th," and "I" is easy for "r," etc. This point as regards Adar, we should say in passing, controls this situation here. If one Babylonian month name was Iranian, it is not sound criticism for us to hold to an isolated occurrence; "many or none" should be our principle. Even if, conceivably, the Iranian month names, all intensely native to Medo-Persian as they are, were later taken over from Babylon after having been previously adapted there from Iran in other applications—even upon the supposition that they, while wholly Iranian, had never before as yet been used in Iran as month names till they had been first so used in Babylon—notwithstanding this so singular presupposition, the fact would remain as clearly proved that these Iranian words had singular power in Babylon at an extremely early date. These considerations taken all together almost make us credit the old opinions of a once paramount semi-Iranian influence in Babylon or in pre-Babylonian times as being intimately associated with the intellectual elements of Akad and Sumer.[6] Arid this, as we should never forget, was also *a priori* more than probable; for Iran could not have developed even to the position occupied by the first Achæmenid except during the course of some centuries and without having made its energetic influence often felt upon neighboring states.

[6] Look at Apsu as plain Iranian; Aps with Semitic nominative suffix. See also Patesi, the name of an Akkadian ruler, Avesta Paitish, etc.

There is one other serious point here which I would introduce as if in parentheses, though it may not seem to be immediately relevant; it is this. Some advanced scholars seem never to have become at all aware of such a fact as that all the Persian Ameshaspends with many of their satellites, whose names are used for the months and the days of the months, were likewise ***Vedic,*** though scattered and not numbered six or seven in the RIK; nor yet at all applied in the same way to the calendar. And this all the more connects the entire body of Iranian religious thought with the great southeastern Indian systems rather than with the southwestern Babylonian, for the Vedic is and was a veritable fellow-branch with the Iranian in one and the same vast primeval faith. But this circumstance also imparts immensely greater solidity to the entire structure of the Iranian religious system, showing it to possess a predominant objectivity, which together with its incisive clearness naturally impressed itself upon its neighbor the Assyrian. As we shall be obliged later on to bring in facts which postdate the New Testamènt and which yet exercise a very important influence upon the issues of this discussion, (see below), we must continue on our preliminary remarks one step further here and refer to some post-Christian elements.

Much additional information of an interior character has been collected by Kohut out of the various early sections of the Talmud, some of it dating so early as before A. D. 226. Prominent among these particulars, and as in analogy with the general Persian atmosphere of the Exile period noted above, would be the favored condition of the Jews under the Parthian Arsacids, which would be available as a point so far back, let us say, as 150 A. D. at least; [7] and perhaps the still more incisive manifestation of

> [7] Their political representative, the Exile arch, ranked fourth after the sovereign. see Kohut's citation.

disfavor under the Sasanids, from 226 A. D. on, may be also highly valued for our purpose, for persecution sometimes[8] brings out details of intellectual connection more sharply even than sympathetic treatment.[9] Next to this and as again parallel to what is above cited, Kohut, with a very fair degree of probability indeed, sees Haur-vatat and Ameretatat in later but still early portions of the Talmud; while the Cinvat Bridge is clearly mentioned somewhere also, though here I can quote only from memory, the very striking particulars of Yasht XXII appear. And what shall we say to the somewhat late but most certain existence of Avesta But, Mush, and the Ashemaogha? Then still later we Have also Talmudic Mittron possibly for Mithra, ur-iel for Hvare-nah, etc., etc.[10] If these items, thus as it were hastily inserted before our more extended discussion, possess any validity at all, then they should already produce an incipient conviction in our minds and so at once begin to make us believe all the acutely interesting and solemn facts involved in the partially approximate identity of the Persian and Israelitish Exilic lores.

After the above preliminary items which I trust may be considered incontestable, as proving ***prima facie*** the con-nection between the Exilic Jewish religious literature and that of the Iranians, the first particular in the division of the subject would be the name and conception of the Supreme Being; then, those of his supernatural personified creatures; the conception of his eternity in general, to-

[8] If not as the general rule.

[9] At the festivals especially held to the Fire the Persian authorities entered the dwellings of the Jews, and put out all the lights; and so at the festivals in honor of the holy waters they deprived them of its use. See Kohut's citations.

[10] Aspiration comes and goes; see Kohut everywhere, "ur-" might well be "Hur"— and this easily "Hvar." Those who criticise Kohut too freely should remember that one has to be a critic to criticise a critic. Much that is sagacious is utterly lost upon non-experts. See "Jüdische Angelologie," ***Ab-hand-lungen fur die Kunde des Morgenlandes,*** Vol. IV, 1866, by A. Kohut See also his successors, N. Soderblom, Ernst Bloken, L. H. Gray, etc.

gether with angelic and human immortality; resurrection; judgment; millennial perfection and heaven; heaven and hell; and finally our conclusions as to what is really Zoro-astrian, and as to what is really Exilic, and as to how far the Hebrew eschatology is original with Israel.

CHAPTER II.

THE CONCEPTION OF GOD AND THE TERMINOLOGY USED.

AMONG the names applied to the Supreme Being the A expression "God of Heaven," also used in the alleged Edicts of Cyrus[11] and his Biblical successors (see 2 Chronicles, Ezra, etc.) appears to be certainly Exilic, even where it may now occur amidst matter formerly believed to be pre-Exilic. It recalls vividly the universal Aryan name Deva,[12] Zeus, Deus, Dieu, etc., for Deity, which in the Aryan vernacular was Divá, "the shining sky,"[13] so D(a)eva, to Indian *div*. In Avesta and its sequents the fine term became unhappily inverted in its application owing to theological antipathies and jealousies, and was actually applied to demons through all Zoroastrian literature. But the Iranians themselves, as there can be little doubt, used "D(a)eva," originally in the holy sense, with all the rest of Arya, and the sad misuse is one proof more of the posteriority even of the early Avesta to the earliest Veda. Then the expression "living God" recalls the etymology of Ahura (Inscriptional Aura) the root being Ahu = "life" *among other things;* -ra is mere suffix. This singularly effective word is indeed applied to Ameshaspends, and even to a human spiritual Lord, and this in the oldest Avesta; but we are none the less entitled to think of "life" and the "living" One when we meet its well-nigh universal

[11] See Ezra i.

[12] So first suggested by me in *T. R. A. S.*

[13] See Daniel

application to the Supreme Deity, recalling also Vedic *sura* and its equivalents (see above). Not long since a scholar would indeed have cited Yahveh as a Jewish analogon; and there is little doubt that the Jews themselves once mistook the word for the first person singular of the Hebrew verb meaning "to be." And this supervening and secondary understanding of the term, entirely aside from our restored modern explanations of it, quite fully suffices to establish an interior, if independent, analogy between it and Ahura. Analogies are often quite valid for the purpose of tracing the presence and connection of ideas here apart even from errors or misgrowths; for "connection" quite as often reveals itself in grotesque anomalies. See even the striking inscriptional expression "King of Kings" applied to God in Hebrew as well as to the Messiah and to Nebuchadnezzar (Daniel ii. 37) ; see it dwelt upon below, whereas in its signal occurrence upon Behistan it is used of Darius; yet this last insertion, though dating so late as B. C. 500, circa, clearly proves that the expression was predominantly Persian in its original application, for it is not possible that it could not have been used in Iran in the course of Iranian history centuries before it was applied in this same sense in the Inscription. And it therefore affords a strong additional proof of a connection of religious ideas. So we hear of the "Ancient of Days," which recalls ***Zrvani akarane,*** meaning "in boundless time": see the Vendidad XIX, an expression of much importance as savoring of philosophic speculation, but at another day (as possibly in the Bible[14]) it becomes a proper name for an Eternal Creator; we have even a sect of Zervanites. Yet this connection, though subjected to a twist, is valid in exactly the same manner, and deeply interesting. Moreover it must be clearly held in mind that a vast mass of analogies must be so estimated while yet cited: see on ahead,

[14] See DanieL

where no pretence whatsoever is to be put forward by me to any certain immediate literary connection. My objective, as already stated, is the existence of a post-Exilic intellectual atmosphere in Persian Babylonia, and so also in Persian Jerusalem, an atmosphere which was vital to the new religious aspirations of the Jews—in fact totally transforming them; and that this atmosphere was more Iranian than Babylonian; but much detail of an otherwise very inferior character goes to make firm our convictions as to this. It is often a question as to what may have circulated as mere hearsay.

Resuming,—we have again a firm clincher to the idea of eternity in the Deity as being an Iranian concept; and this is afforded by the name of the last Ameshaspend, Ameretatat; recall "who only hath immortality"[15] (Timothy vii. 16).

[15] A curious expression for the Bible to make use of. It looks indeed as if "immortality" were a special title; otherwise what is the sense of it at all? Surely it is not a New Testament doctrine that no one but God has "immortality."

CHAPTER III.

ANGELOLOGY WITH DEMONOLOGY.

a. Distinction in Personages.

ANGELIC personages become discriminated as to their A rank as greater or less, in the Exilic and post-Exilic Scriptures, and this marks still further the interesting change in the religious history of Israel. In the genuine pre-Exilic period the angelology was extremely indefinite, having been even thought by some to be a mere theophany, at best a simple messenger-sending from the Deity without the supposition of any very distinct personal charac-eristics in the supernatural messenger himself. We find also naturally little trace of any very exceptional hyper-exaltations of individual angelic or demoniac spiritual beings aside from, and independent of, their use as conveyors of the Divine wishes upon particular occasions. But in the Exile not only are some of these concepts apparently selected to "surround the Throne," but individual beings appear in a most predominant attitude as "Prince" and "Prince of Princes." (See Daniel viii. 25) : An especially prominent angel seems even intended to be represented as the agent in raising the dead, like the Saoshyants[16] of Iran: See Daniel xii. 1, 2: "At that time shall Michael stand up, the great Prince which standeth for thy people." See also the expression "Sons of God" after the Iranian idea

> [16] He was himself not an angel, but the first recorded concept of a final Redeemer restoring all things; see elsewhere and below.

in Yasht XIII and elsewhere where the Iranian Arch-angels "have all one Father Ahura."

Whether the other two in Daniel xii. 5, 6, are to be reckoned as "Princes" is not certain, but the occurrences already mentioned suffice to show an exceptional eminence conceded to an exceedingly small number of these believed-in supernatural persons. Similarly see also Daniel x. 21, where Michael, "Your Prince," almost demands a like interpretation to the expressions "Prince of Persia," (see Daniel x. 13, 20), and even to the expressions "Prince of Grecia." If it is written:

"The Prince of the Kingdom of Persia withstood him, Daniel, one and twenty days,—and, lo,—Michael, one of your Princes, came to help me," then as Michael, the Prince was an Archangel, it would seem only fair for us to suppose that the term "Prince of Persia" may possibly have some inclusive allusion to a supernatural being notwithstanding the positive presence of Persian political personages in the connection; and so the expression "Prince of Grecia" must be somewhat accounted for in the same manner. Of course the word "Prince" here used has also its further and more natural application; and in fact it is quite possible that the entire use of the term "Prince" here as applied to the Archangels may have been first suggested by the necessary mention of the political Princes whose action forms here the subject under discussion. Again, on the contrary, the idea may have been led off by the very prominent position of the national Archangels of Media reckoned as "Princes," a leading one among them having actually the name of Khshathra which maybe rendered "Sovereign" or "Prince"; so that, to be exhaustive, it is desirable to mention that even the "Prince of Grecia" in Daniel x. 13, 20, might point toward a semi-extinct angelology further west; but I fear we should be hardly warranted here.

b. *The Seven Spirits of God.*[17]

It is in Zechariah, Tobit, and Revelations that a few of these more prominent concepts are spoken of as a company of seven; see where I have already necessarily indicated this by anticipation above, and what I shall say here should be regarded as being of the nature of necessary amplification. In the latter book this expression becomes frequent. Nothing could more accord with the Medo-Per-sian Zoroastrian usage, which may also have expressed itself with a prominence which spread and maintained the concepts everywhere within the vast Perso-Babylonian territory.

No one will suppose that I attach any especial importance to the number seven in itself considered, for it is of well-nigh universal application in Holy Scripture, possibly having had its real origin in the seven days of a week in a month of about twenty-eight days; but the application of this number to certain conspicuous believed-in angelic beings is quite another matter when we recall the Medo-Persian Ameshaspends which were so widely known. Here accidental coincidence would seem to be rigorously excluded by the facts which I have already instanced above, for the existence of the expression in close proximity to the name of a Gathic Demon; see above, where an Avesta city more than once in the same document, places connection all the more fully beyond dispute. In Zechariah iv. 10, "the Seven Spirits which are as the eyes of the Lord and which run to and fro throughout the whole earth," not only recall the Seven Ameshaspends, but their activity, which is everywhere expressed, or implied in the Avesta as in the later Zoroastrianism; see also Satan's answer to God in the Introduction to Job, where he says: "I am come from running to and fro in all the earth"; see it cited also

> [17] This is one of the collections of evidence to which I promised to revert, entering into more extended detail.

elsewhere; and we have even the coincidence as to the "eyes of the Lord," the sun being the "eye of Ahura" in Avesta, as he is the eye of Varuna in the Veda; for though the sun was not an Ameshaspend, but merely exalted in a quasi-personification, yet our main object here, as said above, is literary coincidence or color which may be absolutely without interior correspondence and yet completely effective to show "connection."[18] In Rev. viii. 2, we have at once again "the seven spirits which are before the throne." Here the application of the same terms to the seven representatives of the Seven Churches (Rev. i. 20) should hardly be regarded as a serious objection, for these later expressions were evidently taken over from the earlier words, which, as we see, occur in Zechariah and Tobit. It would be moreover *a priori* highly improbable that the "seven spirits of God before His throne" should have been an idea finding its origin in the fact that there were seven Christian Bishops in Asia Minor who attracted the attention of the inspired author; see also below.

Notice moreover the very solemn expression "the seven spirits *of God*" in Rev. iii. 2 and 7, which not remotely recalls the still profounder revelations in the Avesta where an analogous passage attributes the "six" spirits to Ahura as a seventh. This occurrence moreover surpasses its Jewish imitations in one all-important particular; for these spirits were in so far really *God's* (that is to say, Ahura's) that they were literally the fundamental concepts not only of all religion, but of all possible moral existence, and so metaphorically indeed the very "Sons of God"; see below for amplification to this point, being also in a sense absolutely identical with Him, as the human attributes are identical with the human personal subjectivity. As regards Rev. iv. 5 (cp. also Zech. iv. 2, 10) I am not aware that the Zoroastrians had exactly seven lamps, or seven candle-

[18] Compare "the angel who took his part."

sticks, but the concept of the seven spirits pervaded the ideas of the writers, while fire (see above) was supreme as a sacrificial object; see also Rev. v. 7. In 8, the seven angels are again seen to stand before the throne recalling Job, where, however, the number is not mentioned (see Rev. viii. 6; xv- 1; xv. 6; xvi. 17; xvii. 11; xx. 19). The same deduction is everywhere in point, namely that while the concepts with their number "seven" are so very Jewish and Christian, they only appeared suddenly upon this Hebrew foreign soil as applied to particular personal spirits, whereas *they were immemorially native to Medo-Persian Zoroastridnism* which for centuries occupied the same territory which was both before and later by constraint invaded by the captives.[19] A further explanation of this crucial number seven should here intervene, and it will afford an all-important illustration as to the asserted facts upon which our entire procedure depends. For, like almost every other particular of the kind, it is not expected to go upon "all fours." Even the number itself wobbles, the seven being a post-Gathic term, as is indeed the word ***amesha,*** (better ***amersha***), meaning "immortal," as applied to the Seven; and it, the number seven, first of all includes Ahura. The Ameshaspentas without Him are merely six, whereas in one of the most important of all the passages, the Seven are all said to have "One Father," Ahura. But such irrationalities are universal in ancient religious literatures. The number seven struck its impression deep upon the Iranian mind, having its obvious origin in the number of the Ameshas (Immortals) with Ahura included, and once having gained a footing it twisted their terminology. The word seems later to have meant the Holy Group entirely aside from the actual accuracy of the figure.

That the names or the personified ideas themselves

[19] The places where the Israelitish captives were deposited and settled were "Assyria and the Cities of the Medes."

were purposely selected by the original authors to fit in with the already established sanctity of the number is less probable than ***vice versa,*** from the facts already just noticed ; there is no idea of "seven" at all in the original doc-uments, the Gathas. We might indeed surmise that an originally prevailing sanctity of such a number among the Irano-Aryan tribes, having returned more vividly to the consciousness of the later Zoroastrians, and also possibly having found its way in from without, they may then in the later but still genuine Avesta have adopted the term, fitting it into the fact that the "Six" with their Original, were indeed "Seven"; recall the Seven Karsh-vas,—but the probabilities lie totally on the other side of it. The sanctity of the Six with Ahura, the Seventh, or as the First of a Seven, was of the most exalted and effective character possible, affording among the Iranians at least and their descendants whether actual or merely intellectual, an all-sufficient reason for the excessive veneration for the number, as usual on rational grounds; for what reasons for the sanctification of any such figure could at all approach the fact that it expressed the number of the accepted, or recognized attributes of the Supreme Deity? And even if the glimmer of the idea of Seven did indeed revive from an earlier Iranian-Indian origin, or even, if it did later creep in from abroad; yet even then it was obviously, notoriously, and almost exclusively appropriated by the unconscious facts of the Iranian theological situation. No one who reads the Gathas with any receptive capacity at all could imagine that those Six were especially worked out to coincide with the superficial and indeed artificial sanctity of any number elsewhere super-stitiously adored. If that had been the case Seven would undoubtedly have been mentioned in them, the Gathas. If the number "seven" had any very especial sanctity in the pre-Gathic period that sanctity may have been purposely nursed from religious motives, and it may have exerted a quiet influence even in the Gathic period, but in no degree such a powerful and dominant influence as it exerted in all subsequent Iranian history.

Nothing is more pressingly important to all our constructive conjectures than to recall this principle at every step. Hardly an item, except these first cited, presents a mechanically exact correspondence. Another excellent example should be noted merely for the sake of emphasizing our illustration. Aramaiti is rhetorically termed "God's daughter" in several places, and "His wife" in another. So Mithra is almost His fellow-God at times, and yet His creature at others. In more than one place Ahura actually sacrifices to Mithra and others of His sub-deities, just as a courteous sovereign would never formally address a nobleman without using his title. Ancient Gods also universally borrow each other's attributes, and in pursuing scientific discriminations as to these points the expert must note which god is predominant in the possession of certain characteristics. Periods of transition also occur during which each leading god usurps or inherits the accredited deeds or powers of the others; and there are often distinctly marked epochs, where One God, as represented by his followers, seems almost to wrangle for an attribute with a waning predecessor.[20]

Periods of the prevailing ascendency of one God also overlap upon those of another.

c. The Naming of the Archangels.

While such a culmination was most possible as an entirely independent Jewish growth in parallel lines with that in the Zoroastrian scriptures, yet in presence of the immemorial Avestic and Vedic use, one at once recognizes the influence of the new Persian scene. The

[20] See Indra as he supplants his predecessors in R. V.

Jews, being Persian subjects, were perforce upon the most intimate political terms with many of the Persian officials, and they could not meet and converse religiously with any Persian - Babylonian acquaintance from Media, without hearing at every sentence the name of an Archangel, for these fine believed-in supernatural personages later gave the very names to the months and days,[21] and this usage may well have begun at a date which would here come in; and they were often used in the course of the day in private devotion. Their names also occurred often in private proper names, the Greeks themselves becoming aware of them (see below). What wonder then that they began, though at first quite unconsciously, not only to con-struct intellectually their own personified religious concepts, and upon the same model as those of the Iranians (see above), but to name them as well, after the same fashion which was ever upon the lips of their political and social allies.

"The man Gabriel being caused to fly swiftly," etc. (Daniel) may be taken as a leading illustration. The few Zoroastrian "Immortals," unlike even their first imitations in Zech. iv, dispense with the supernatural limbs of locomotion, and especially with contra-anatomical growths for aerial excursion, but Gabriel, "Man of God," at once recalls the fact that Vohumanah represents precisely "the man of God" even in the Gathas, not etymologically of course; and in the Vendidad he represents him in a manner so emphatic that there Vohu Manah, as representing the well-conducted citizen, may even be "defiled" through some impure physical contamination (see below); and we

[21]Not only were many of the months named after them and their underlings; but the days of the month as well. Everything rang with the terms, so to speak, not excepting sometimes the proper names of the most eminent persons; for instance in such a word as Artaxerxes we have the names of two of the immortals, — Arta, which equalled Asha, and Khshathra; the prayer hours of the day, later five m number involved the constant recalling of the names.

should not fail to add that the Zoroastrian angels have also a "flight" in descending to the believer, but as ever in the more refined form of rhetorical imagery rather than in that of muscular delineation.[22] So when the leading priests in Persian Babylon began to think out for themselves Archangelic personages they would naturally give some such names as we have recorded; and so Michael "who like God?" appeared. We have noticed Gabriel as recalling Vohuman; but he also recalls the exploits of many an Iranian Angel, Sraosha in particular, though he, Sraosha, was certainly not at first recognized as an Amesha, yet he succeeded in pushing some of these leading forms aside in his progress as a defender. So in Revelations there was "war" in heaven and Michael the Prince contended with the Devil in Jude, just as Sraosha pre-eminently vanquished Angra-Mainyus. But we must not go further before we recall and further explain the incisive circumstance that the Zoroastrian names differ radically and transcend immensely the Biblical ones in an all-important particular, already touched upon above, for whereas the Jewish expressions depict with color fine poetical images, the Zoroastrian terms express the first internal elements of the mental universe; see above and in the following remarks. ***Vohu manah,*** while used for the "orthodox saint," means distinctly ***bona mens;*** they may be the same words indeed in another form; ***manah*** is of course mens. Asha is "the law," the "idea of consecutive order," the "truth pre-emi-nent" in every germ; Khshathra, the sovereign power, comes in also as if with conscious logic; compare both the Gathic and the Lord's prayer ;[23] in the first we have "Thine is the kingdom," as in the last, with no very probable immediate literary connection; it is the idea of sacred authoritative force; Aramaiti is the psychic energy of purpose,

[22] Yt. xiii. 84, 84.

[23] See Yasna LIII, 7: "For 'thine is the kingdom' through which Thou wilt

give to the right-living poor."

"the toiling Mind,"[24] while Haurvatat is the completeness of Deity, conferring full weal and chiefly health upon His "good" creatures, and Ameretatat is literally "immortality," the two forms of exactly the same word. As approaching this we have such expressions as "The Amen"; see the Asha = Truth. Descending to the minor concepts; see above my allusions to "Hvarenah," etc. In addition to this we may recall the fact that Raphael, one of the Jewish Archangels, is actually declared to be "One of the Seven Spirits" in the Tale of Tobit which almost centers about the chief Zoroastrian city Ragha.

d. Iranian Names Suggested Where Neither They Nor Any Semitic Equivalents Actually Appear.

While Michael and Gabriel are in evidence on the Semitic side and "God of Heaven" has been cited as possibly an Aryan element amidst the throng of Semitic terms, we may proceed to notice such an expression as that in Daniel ii. 11, "whose dwellings are not in the flesh." This would be an advance upon earlier concepts where the bodily figure of Yahveh Elohim is plainly referred to; and these finer ideas arose under the stimulus of the Exile, anthropomorphic modes of thought having been much shaken off, not necessarily at all in imitation of Persian modes of expression. For even in the Gathas, a vision of Ahura is sought for, though a vision of Ahura as manifested in a bodily form would indeed introduce an element into the Gathas directly in conflict with one of its leading distinctions, that between the "bodily" and the "mental" worlds. In the later Yasna, however, we have His "Body," though everything points to a merely rhetorical (xx. 2) usage here as in the post-Avestic Zoroastrianism, though I do not feel that the post-Gathic Zoroastrians would have objected much to God's body, if they could only have managed the idea of it; and it

[24] I refer ar to ar = "to plough" cp. ***aratrum.***

would have been easy enough to add the adjective "spiritual" before such a noun as "body." A "God of Gods" (Daniel ii. 47) recalls again the inscriptional turn of words "King of Kings" and also its actual sentence "greatest of all the Gods," the Creator both of the Immortals and of Mithra; see below. Strangely enough Adar, the angel of fire, is most significantly indicated in Daniel iii. 25: "The fourth figure walking in the super-heated furnace is like unto a son of the gods." But "Son of God," i. e., of Ahura, was precisely a most noted and ever iterated title of the fire, as somewhat dimly personified in the later but still genuine Avesta. The spirit of the Holy Gods, in Daniel iv. 9, recalls again the Spenishta Mainyu, the most Holy Spirit, so the most; I prefer, the "most August Spirit." In the Avesta this "most August Spirit" is a curious growth out of the concept Ahura, much like that of the Holy Spirit in the Exilic Scriptures. It seems to be a sort of attribute at first; and then perhaps it edged its way into personification, as so often with similar ideas. The "watcher and the Holy One" of Daniel iv. 13 suggest Sraosha who "never slept since the two Spirits made the worlds; three times of the night and day" he attacks the enemy and defends the souls of the faithful. The "coming down from Heaven" (same verse) suggests the Six in Yasht XIII, where we have, "shining are their paths as they come down to the faithful." In Daniel iv. 17, the demands "by the words of the Holy Ones" again suggest the Seven; they all, constructively, watch and speak; and see "the Spirit of the Holy Gods" again with "Spenishta Mainyu" as its counterpart.

The reader has long since, let us hope, fully seen the pointing of our procedure. While hardly a single instance here cited shows any absolutely certain immediate and definite external literary connection with Avesta, yet ***the duty continually grows upon us to gather up not only the more prominent evidences of interior connection arising from parallel development, but the entire mass of them; for they undoubtedly accumulate force if only slowly,*** and they build up a structure of comparative theological doctrine which demands a universal recognition; and as it gains a hearing, it gradually but surely substantiates the Zoroastrian-Israelitish historical connection as well. To resume—see "the watchers" like Sraosha again at Daniel iv. 23. The talk of "the kingdoms" is again original, and yet it again suggests

Avesta Khshathra; see by anticipation the "care of the poor"[25] (iv. 27) cited from the Gathas above and below. This idea occurs more than once in the Gathas and also in the Ahuna Vairya. The "most high ruling" suggests "Ahura as king." See the "Spirit of the Holy Gods" still once more again in Daniel iv. 34. In v. 20 "the Glory taken away" from the monarch, suggests the Hvarenah of the Kavis as elsewhere. This latter, however, eluded seizure; see the Yashts. The **word Satraps**[26] of vi.7 is pure Persian of course; cp khshathrapa-van, though the Archangel Khshathra was not here at all directly thought of.

The "Living God" (vi. 26) again suggests the same thoughts which originally determined the word Ahura; see above. See also "The Ancient of Days" again, which, aside from that most significant expression "in Boundless Time"[27] recalls Ahura as he who is "the same at every now" ; recall "the same, yesterday, to-day and for ever."[28] All the expressions in vii. 14 recall the Spirit of the new Persian - Babylonian religious thought, "indestructible kingdom" being also familiar to both. Most curiously both

[25]The "care of the poor" was a marked Gathic idea; and in spite of a despotic government, if not in consequence of it, the "poor" seem always to have had some special privileges in Persia as against the aristocracy.

[26]Darius's father was one of his son's Satraps.

[27] Recall the Greek Chronos.

[28] See above where "Boundless Time" itself became a deity and a creator.

the ram and the he-goat of 8, appear in the Yasht to Vic-tory, a brilliant Avesta piece, and likewise in the same order, with the ram first. Notice Gabriel's, "the man's voice," of viii. 16, the Prince of Princes of viii. 25 which ought always to suggest Vohu Manah, while Asha, who secured the first place among the Archangels, was later, as already stated, rudely pushed off the stage of action by Sraosha who is also elsewhere metaphorically aggres-sive, "Righteousness belongeth unto Thee," originally arose from the same impulsive convictions which attributed Asha, the

Holy Legal Truth, to Ahura. So Vohu-manah was really "mercy"; see ix. 9. In ix. 10, "not obeying" arose from the same psychic forces which evoked the condemnation of **ascroasha**, non-obedience in Y, LX, 9,11. There was also a "curse" almost personified in Avesta. "The Lord watching over evil" (ix. 14) recalls Isaiah xiv. 7, in contradiction to the implication that God did not 'create sin, while, on the contrary, Ahura was thus limited. See again "all the Righteousness of God," (ix. 16), recalling the Asha of Ahura.

"Hearken, hear, and incline Thine ear," (ix. 18), are emphatic and iterated Gathic ideas and words, and the first conception of Sraosha is "God's ear." So are "hear and forgive" ;[29] so also "bringing in everlasting righteousness" (Daniel ix. 24) is very Avestic as the first essential idea of **Frashakart**[30] without which the supernatural beatifications comprised within that engaging hope would be of no effect; cp. "no envy Demon-made." Daniel x: the Yashts are full of "war"[31] as are indeed the Gathas, these last have however no pictorial personifications to correspond. I cannot say what Aryan angel is suggested by "the man clothed in linen," though as already said, Vohumanah,

[29] Y. XXXII, 11.

[30] Millennial Perfection .

[31] Cp. Yt XIX, I, where Ahura himself takes part.

representing "man," recalls Gabriel. In x. II, "He comes" like Vohuman, so repeatedly in Y. XLIII; see x. 18, the same motives inducing both descriptive manifestations. In xi. 2 the "truth" is again Asha.

In xi. 16 "doing according to His will" emphatically recalls the very characteristic and repeated expression of Avesta, "using power according to His will"; see also the **vasiy**[32] of the Inscription; see also Khshathra again as the "Divine Rule" (xi. 17). I do not know what to suggest with regard to the other two angels of Daniel xii. 5.

e. Unnamed Semitic Angels With Aryan Analogies.

The Angel in Rev. i who leads and conducts the narrator was suggested by the same idea as determined Sra-osha to a similar office in the Book of the Arta-i-Viraf of the later Zoroastrianism; see also Y. XXVIII, **5**, of the Gathas; so "in the spirit" (Rev. i. 10) is very Zoroastrian, though not exactly in the pointed sense. Arta-i-Viraf, however, was "in the spirit" much after the fashion of St. John, though in his case (Arta-i-Virafs) this took place with the assistance of a drug. There is also a prominent book called the "Spirit of Wisdom."

"Writing in a book" reminds us that Zoroastrianism with Judaism was one of the very few prominent book-religions. The Son of Man again, as in Daniel, recalls Vohuman who represented "man."[33] In Rev. i. 16, the "sword from the mouth" suggests the weapon of Sraosha which was emphatically "the Word of God," the Honover of Avesta.[34] In Rev. i. 17, "the first and the last" sounds like a keynote of the Avesta, though there the Devil shared this primordial eternal existence. There were "two first spirits": see also the word ap(a)ourvyam, "having no first"; that is to

[32] Meaning "at will," "with complete sway."

[33] See above.

[34] SeeYasnaXIX.

say, "having none before it," which qualifies the superex-cellence of the chants; see below on the "new song." Yet some expositors might well apply the term grammatically to Mazda Ahura. In Rev. i. 18 the "Living One" again recalls Ahu-ra; see above, here, however, apparently referring to the risen Jesus, whereas in Daniel the Deity is held in view.

The description of the seven stars as the "seven angels of the seven churches (Rev. i. 20) by no means annihilates, but rather on the contrary assists our contention as to the analogies. The idea and the words as already stated, were taken over from the seven angels before "the throne." The reversed direction would be quaint indeed.[35] The human Angels were addressed in the terms of common parlance. "I know thy works" (ii. 2) expresses the essence of Zoro-astrian judgment; see the first strophe of the Gathas. The "tree of life" (ii. 7) reminds one of Ameretatat, which represented both never dying life, and later the vegetable kingdom which supported it, whereas in Genesis it recalls the vine with its supposed supernatural excitations, for which compare the Horn Yasht which celebrates the same sacred influence, "he that hath an ear to hear" (ii. 11) is again so significant in the Avesta that it has an especial angel, Sraosha, to represent it; see also the Yasna, where "Hear ye these things with the ears," twice introduces the most solemn and far-reaching of all the doctrines. He who was dead and is alive again" (Rev. ii. 8), recalls the realization of the ideas which lurk in Ameretatat and are expressed fully elsewhere; see below. The intervention of the Satanic opposition (ii. 9) is everywhere marked in Zoroastrianism, where it was first recognized; but the details of the Semitic allusions are here the most pointed.

[35] As if the idea of "the seven spirits of God" was derived from the idea of the seven Bishops.

Periods of trial (ii. 10) are familiar throughout Zoro-astrianism, and the key-note of all is final victory, certainly at least for the elect. "The crown of life" (ii. 10) is far more poetical than the mere immortality of the Avesta, though victory abounds in the latter. Satan's throne (ii. 13) is not positively an Avestic expression; but the counterparts to Vendidad XIX, 32 (105), and Yasht XXII, have been lost; there "evil" thrones are due to offset the holier ones. We are also reminded of the top of Arezura, V. XIX. 45 (w) where the choice of spirits of the infernal world converge, doubtless under the presidency of their chief. In Rev. ii. 13, "Satan's dwelling" recalls strikingly the abode of the Druj, Y. XLVI, XLIX, the Devil's eldest daughter, almost himself. Idol-worship (ii. 14) is one of the chief things condemned at the judgment of the Zoroas-trians. In ii. 17, the "Spirit" recalls again the "most Holy," or "August Spirit" of the Gathas exactly in analogy with the Holy Spirit of the Old and New Testaments, with no immediate literary connection. The hidden manna, (Rev. ii. 17) also somewhat dimly recalls the immortal food of the Zoroastrian "Heaven," the Holy Oil of the beatified. "The Son of God," who has "eyes like a flame of fire" and feet like "burnished" and so "fiery brass" again recalls our Adar also represented in Avesta under the rhetorical image of personification. And we notice once again that the fire was "God's son," the expression often occurring. Rev. ii. 19, again recalls the first verse of the Gatha, "all works done with Asha." Both Zoro-astrianism and Rev. ii. 20 are severe upon the harlot. In ii. 23, one "which searcheth the heart" recalls "on all with the truth (i. e., searchingly) Thou art gazing." The "Son of God" as "benevolent" sympathy (Rev. ii. 19) recalls the noted expression in the Gathas, "with Asha in sympathy," as also that which reports "the love of Ahura Mazda." "The depths of Satan" (ii. 24) recall the "things hidden" of Yasna XXXI. "Behold I come quickly" (Rev. ii. 16) recalls the Gathic expression "swift be it" (the issue) as addressed to Ahura. Here we have as so often no immediate literary connection, but the two ideas were determined by the same psychological moment.

Vohumanah distinctly recalls the "beginning of the creation of God" (iii. 14) as he was supposed to be the "first[36] made of every creature," not, however, an Avestic expression. See the "Amen" again for Asha in a most solemn and heart-touching sense from interior parallel development.

"He that overcometh" (Rev. iii. 21) is again very Zor-oastrian of "Victory." In iii. 21, the sitting upon the throne again recalls the scene in the Vendidad. The four and twenty elders on thrones (iv. 4) or round about the throne are exactly the Immortals in Vendidad though the number there in V. is but a fourth of them; see below. Vohu Manah seems to sit down, if not *with* Ahura on His throne, V. XIX, 132 (105), yet upon a throne in His near vicinity; recall where the Son of Man sits upon the throne of His Glory (Vohu Manah also representing the religious man in Avesta, as to which see below); the Deity also presumably presided. So the seven lamps of fire, (4, 5) have been already mentioned as a manifestation of the angel Atar (Adar). In iv. 6 the living creature full of eyes seems distinctly motived by Mithra with his 1000 eyes (see also Ezekiel). The especial homage to God as "the Creator" (iv. 11) is perhaps more constantly present in Zoroastrianism than in any other lore (see also the In-scriptions). "Glory" in iv. 11 again recalls Hvarenah and its angel; see Power equalling Khshathra again. "Because of thy will" (iv. 11) is again very Avestic and in-scriptional both as applied to Ahura and His saints.

[36] Vohumanah worked his way to the fore on account of his meaning which was "Benevolence."

"Power" is again Khshathra (v. 12). "Riches" is Ashi Vanguhi; "wisdom" may be Aramaiti; "glory" again is Hvarenah. The "white horse" of vi. 2 is a striking symbol in the Yasht to victory; see also "conquering and to conquer." The "bow" was pre-eminently the Persian weapon, baffling the Romans in many an encounter,[37] the "horse that was red" (vi. 4) recalls again the Avesta with the varying color; and so the "black horse" (vi. 5), all presumably in the sky, or on some conspicuous elevation. The angel of the Abyss (ix. 11) is Angra Mainyu, or his agent, ("face downward are the D(a)evas"). Recall Ezek. viii. 16 and the "twenty-five men with their backs to the temple as they worshiped the sun," pure Zoroastrianism, or the like. The "beast coming up out of the abyss," (Rev. xi. 7) recalls again the demon Angra Mainyu, who among his myrmidons certainly fled to Hell, which was situated in a downward direction; see in Vendidad; see also Arta-i-Viraf. "After three days and a half" (xi. 9) vividly recalls the idea of the period during which the soul lingers around the body in Yasht, XXII; see also the approximately similar borrowed Muhammedan belief. (It would seem to be profane to mention the "three days" of the Gospels.)

Passing over much interesting and apposite detail we have in Rev. xii. 7 the "war in Heaven," elsewhere also often mentioned, which precisely in this connection recalls the war of Apaosha in the Yasht, whose enemy was then as now well thought to be drought, the great enemy of man in torrid climates; this point in Avesta is again rational.

"The Deceiver of the world" (xii. 9) is beyond all doubt a Zoroastrian idea of the Devil, whose central product was the Lie-Druj (female demon). "The kingdom of our God" (xii. 10) recalls again of course "Thine is the

[37] The supply of arrows was furnished in camel loads and almost inex-

haustible.

kingdom" in the Gatha; the expression of Royal authority **par eminence,** is Khshathra. This "Reign of God" is again pre-eminently Khshathra who was Ahura's attribute: "the temple of God which is in heaven" (xi. 19) recalls the same idea of celestial supernatural architecture in Avesta. The dragon of seven heads is, of course, the Azhi Dahaka of Avesta, the Ahi of the Veda, which both had six heads, the six being changed to seven in Revelation on account of the dominant influence of that number with possible reference to the Seven Hills of Rome.

Like the Vedic Ahi, he kept off the rain.[38] "The Devil having great wrath" (xii. 12) vividly reminds us of Aeshma, the demon of the **Raid Fury,** again quite a rational concept. There was also "an eagle" in the Avesta in the Yasht (xii. 14). The "worship of the dragon" (xiii. 4) was literally again suggested by that of the great rational Azhi Dahaka (see also the Veda) who showed his claim to be the greatest of the devils, coiling his folds about the rain clouds, the dripping cows of heaven. The "angel with the eternal Gospel" (xiv. 7) is the Sraosha with the Manthra; so only in strongest analogy, of course.

In xiv. 18, the angel who had power over fire is again distinctly an Atar whether directly and immediately so suggested, or by parallel development. In xv. 3, the "King of the Ages" again recalls **Zrvana akarana.** "Boundless Time," which became a Deity; see the sect of the Zervan-ites already more than once noticed.

At xvi. 3, the angel that poured into the sea recalls the Gospatshah of the Mainyu-i-Khard. In xvi. 13, the "unclean spirits like frogs" strikingly recall the fact that the frog was perhaps the most prominent among unclean beasts in Avesta. And let me also say here in passing that

[38] Notice in passing what I must refer to later on, which is the constant rationalism of the Avesta-Vedic concepts as against the Babylonian-Israelitish. One of the most marvelous of literary circumstances is that all the gods, or most of them, have meaning in Avesta, as in Veda and for the most

part abstract meaning.

the Avesta alone affords rational explanation of the distinction between clean and unclean, from the fact that the Devil made the latter. Many animals (like indeed the very ones here in question, the frogs) were quite harmless except as regards some nocturnal voicings, and even used as choice food in some localities; but they were ostracized from the "pure creation," and solely because ***their creator was the Iranian Satan.***

Notice again the "Lord of Lords and King of Kings" (xvii. 14). The "angel having great authority" (xviii. 1) is again a fine Khshathra, Ahura's Sovereign Power. The angel "with the great mill-stone" recalls the mythical Zoroaster who assaults the enemy with an enormous piece of rock;"large as a cottage," so some render. The Amen (xix. 4) is again always a good Asha, Ahura's "Law and Truth." In xix. 6, we have Ahura reigning, in 7, again the glory, Hvarenah. The "marriage of the Lamb" (xix. 9) recalls the figurative concept of the "wives of God," and again, the sacred feast of the Zoroastrian heaven. In xix. 11, we have a rare bit of Zoroastrian drawing. The "white horse" once more immediately suggests again the "white steed" of the Yasht to victory; see also the four-span white horses of Sraosha. The "faithful and true" one recalls the old Persian ideal (see Herodotus) ; it had its root in Asha. The "word of God" is again the Honover which was "before the world," and "the sword by which His angel slays" the Devil, so Zoroaster repels him in his "temptation" with it. The name upon his thigh is again pur Aryan "King of Kings" of the Inscriptions, here fitting in especially because not applied to the Supreme Deity, as indeed also once in Daniel where as in the Persian Inscription it refers to a human potentate. In xix 17, we have the Hvare Khsh(a)-eta as the shining sun once more; recall again Ezekiel viii. 16, with "the five and twenty who, turning their backs to the temple, worshiped the sun." The Ezekiel passages cannot be called pre-Exilic, nor, if they were genuinely of his date, can they be said to rank the Daric Inscriptions, which were supposed to be somewhat later; for, while it is absolutely certain that the allusion to the sun-worshipers was motived by foreign influence upon the Jews, the expressions upon the Inscriptions as positively prove that they had long pre-existing native predecessors; or that they were even stereotyped formulas; see whole sentences mathematically repeated in the Inscriptions on Behistan and on those elsewhere which were later than Darius. This proves almost conclusively that Darius's terms were formulas long since used also by his predecessors as well, so that an inscriptional expression necessarily implies an earlier original in Iran; but the same argument does not hold with regard to the terms in Ezekiel to prove a prior Israelitish origin, because these latter were *distinctly of foreign origin.* We can not say in regard to those of Israel, as we can say of those of Behistan, that these ideas in Ezekiel must have had predecessors in Israel. For it seems to be distinctly acknowledged by all fair-minded and capable persons that the general cast of ideas as regards the eschatology and its kindred points existing in the time of the Exile and subsequently to it, was strikingly different from the tone of thought upon these subjects in the earlier Biblical literature. "Satan being bound a thousand years" (xx. 3, 5) rests broadly upon Zoroastrian Chiliasm; see Plutarch's account of it; see also the later Bundahesh which is a pure development from the earliest documents; see also below. The expression "a thousand years" occurs more than three times in the Avesta itself, and all the other features are likewise marked in it. Recall also the expressions cited by Plutarch from Theo-pompus(?).

The "Throne of God and of the Lamb" (xxii. 1) again recalls Ahura's throne with Vohu Manah. The angel sent to show the revelation (xxii. 8) again recalls Sraosha both in Yasna XXVIII and in the Arta-i-Viraf. "The pure river of the water of life" (xxii. i) makes us think at once of *Ardvi sura Anahita,* "the river lofty, heroic, (i. e., effective), and the spotless which purified all seed, and all generative production ;" see also the other holy waters so constantly in evidence. Without laying the smallest stress upon any possible or probable immediate literary connection showing the influence of the Avesta in the above particulars cited from Ezekiel, Zechariah, Daniel and the Apocalypse, it is yet difficult to resist the conviction from the whole of them, that they conjointly indicate the intellectual and esthetic world in which the Exilic and post-Exilic Jews and Jewish Christians lived; and that this was dominated by the scenes and associations of the Perso-Baby-lonian Exilg But the Perso-Babylonian intellectual world was interpenetrated with the same type of conception and imagery which previously, or simultaneously, prevailed in the Median Zoroastrianism and in the religion of the Daric Achæmenian inscriptions; and the "captive exiles" are twice pointedly said to have been re-settled in the "Cities of the Medes" as well as in Assyria. If this were the case the priests of the people were in almost daily contact with highly ritualistic Zoroastrians or pre-Zoroastrians, if I might so express myself, Zoroastrianism being of course only a culmination. Even had they never met the Median priests, which is well-nigh impossible, the main tenets of Zoroastrianism were daily forced upon their notice through the laity, who had later five periods in the day for reciting prayers, and may have had them earlier. Here then was "contact" and in pre-eminence.

CHAPTER IV.

THE CONCEPT OF ETERNITY IN GENERAL.

THIS is now a convenient place for us to pause and recall the main Jewish Exilic and the Zoroastrian concepts of eternity in general, more closely considering them as applied to the supposed existence of the supernatural beings above discussed. As we have already conceded, the pre-Exilic concepts of futurity were extremely indistinct, but under the general inspiration of the Exile the other life began to take on its now familiar marked characteristics; see above. This has been our result so far

Prominent among the expressions used would be "for ever and ever"; see Daniel ii. 4; ii. 44; the New Testament needs not to be cited. So that we have before us an entirely fresh *Dogmatik* as to this particular in their Exilic and post-Exilic documents

But in the Avesta we have an "endless futurity" from the remotest inception of the lore and we have also in it, as we may well claim, the earliest expression of the idea in a refined literature and outside of barbaric assertions of it. J This occurs in the oldest Avesta in such terms as *vispai yavoi,* "to all futurity," *yavaetaite,* "in the continuance, i. e., forever," as well as in the entire build and organic unity of the works which substantiate our claim for the Avesta that it is the first document of this concept. "Immortality" of another kind must have been thought of times without number wherever the human race appeared; recall the common visions of the dead in cerebral hyper-action, as in dreams. In our natural anxiety to do justice to the initiative of the Avesta upon this particular, we must by no means make light of this.

Unquestionably indeed the thought of immortality in the Veda first acquired consistency from that of "long life" only, the "hundred autumns" of the Rik. The fact that the word for it is literally "immortality," **Ameretatat,** the identical term, differing only in the suffix (see above), should by no means however decide the matter for us, as a beginner might so naturally suppose; for mere "long life" in this world, was certainly expressed by such a word as "non-death," just as by a curious anomaly "eternity" was, on the contrary, at times expressed by a word literally merely "long-life" as in the Veda; and there is some doubt that the term **dirgh-ayu**—or read **dirghayo**—does not mean "Thou eternal" after all in the Gatha; see Y. XXVIII. Be this all in the fact of it as it may, the idea is constructively applied even in the Gathas to Ahura as well as to His saints, and must therefore in such connections mean "long eternal life"[39] while in the next oldest book, the Haptang-haiti, the term **Amesha** (better **Amersha,** i. e., "immortal"; see above), is directly applied to the Archangels, in which case this word Ameretatat must certainly mean at times something very different from "old age." As to human immortality, see everywhere; but as to the more pointed particulars of the subject, see below.

[39] Certainly in Yasht, XIII, 83, where Ameretatat has Ahura as her father.

CHAPTER V.

RESURRECTION.

ASIDE from the actual occurrence of such ideas as the A number seven when applied to the Archangels of the Avesta and to those mentioned in the Exilic Semitic documents above cited, together with the other similar matters noted, nothing has been considered more effective for the establishment of analogies between the Exilic Bible and the Avesta than the passage Daniel xii. "Many of them that sleep in the dust of the earth shall awake, some to everlasting life, and some to shame and everlasting contempt."

The antecedent passage to it is in Isaiah xxvi. 19, and the strongest sequent is that of the well-known place in Rev. xx. 12. This recalls at once a dominant element in Zoroastrianism.

a. Resurrection in the Gatha.

In the Gathas attention is rather turned to human immortality in the light of accountability, making them the earliest consistent documents of such a belief in a civilized literature, while corporeal resurrection is for the most part only implied throughout, as if it were regarded as a secondary matter. See, however, the expression "forever in the Druj's home their bodies lie." Here my colleagues, however, have laudably suggested another cast of meaning—"forever they are citizens of the Druj's abode." But the Sanskrit *ast'i* which renders an ast'ayah (= "bodies") probable, corresponds well with Avesta astayo (ast'ayah) ="bodies," and "bodies," i. e., "persons." "Bodies in the house" is, I think, a more probable rendering than "citizens," particularly as the Druj's abode is equivalent to "Hell." "Citizens" of itself is a "good" term in Avesta just as the word for "augmentation" of itself almost im-plies "holiness," in ancient Parsi conceptions. "Citizens of Hell" is not therefore of itself a natural Avestic expression; for without further explanation we should understand the word "citizen" to imply normal good character,[40] so that my rendering above cited remains the most rational, and affords us the idea of "bodies" in the future world as does the later but still genuine Avesta; moreover, the evil souls receive evil food, endure darkness, hear evil speech, all of which, unless wholly figurative, implies bodily organs ; and last of all it is a law of exegesis that the most objective rendering should be first suggested.

The Frashakart in the Gatha, like the idea, of the Ame-shaspends, is so real, that it, like them,[41] has not yet secured a quasi-technical name there; so that we cannot pointedly bring it in; but this signal group of thoughts interpreted by the later Avesta implies a corporeal resurrection.

"May we be like those who bring on this world's perfection," alludes to the future millennial or ultimate beatific state, as to which see below.

b. Resurrection in the Later Avesta.
In the later Avesta we lose the dignity of the Gatha, but we gain more detail and color; see such passages as

> [40] This is a distinction of the utmost critical importance. Many expressions in ancient books so notoriously convey the impression that the ideas involved in them were of themselves "favorable" and "affirmative" that we are almost at times constrained to restore an apparently improbable text in a sense adapted to this important characteristic
>
> [41] The terms ***Amesha spent a*** do not occur in the Gathas, appearing first in the next earliest pieces.

"we sacrifice to the Kingly Glory which shall cleave unto the victorious Saoshyant (the One about to benefit, or to 'save') when he shall make the world progress unto perfection."

Note again that this passage, although considered to be "late," has not yet reached that period when this last idea of "progress to perfection" was represented by an especial name, a technical "Fraskakart"; for it is again clothed in language which still possesses internal significance of a fully vital character; as much so as in the fresh-making" of Yasna XXX. See Yasht XIX for the further form and color, "where it, the world, shall be never dying, not decaying, never rotting, ever living, ever useful (profit-making), having power to fulfil all wishes [a characteristic expression, meaning that 'the world's inhabitants will then be dominant'], when the dead shall arise and immortal life[42] shall come, when the settlements shall all be deathless." See also fragment V of Westergaard: "Let Angra Mainyu, the Evil Spirit be hid beneath[43] the earth; —let the D(a)evas disappear;—let the dead arise, and let bodily life be sustained in these now lifeless bodies." No-tice the absolute impossibility of merely "old age" as the meaning of "immortal" here.

c. In the Later Zoroastrianism.

In the Bundahesh, chap. XXXI, we have as follows :[44] "On the nature of the resurrection it says in Revelations

> [42]This passage has always been held by thorough scholars to follow the Gathas by a few centuries, but a tendency has been lately manifested to place the later Avesta some centuries after Christ, and this while the Gath-as themselves are still firmly held to be at least somewhat older than the Achæmenian inscriptions. But this would be to place a vast interval of time, more than a thousand years, between the original Avesta and its sequents, which seems to me to be rather irrational. The later Zoroastrianism is how-ever a different matter. That of course post-dated the later Avesta, which intervenes between it, the later Zoroastrianism, and the Gathas.
>
> [43] Notice that Hell was downward.
>
> [44] See *S. B. E.t* VoL V, pp. 120 ff.

(referring formally, as we see, to once pre-existing documents as current lore....) that... .in the millennium of Hushedarmah (a supernaturally born posthumous son of Zarathushtra) the strength of appetite will diminish; they will first desist from meat and then from milk, then from water; and for ten years before Saoshyans they remain without food and do not die."

We notice at once the degeneration in the delineation from the terms of the genuine but later Avesta, how much more from that of the Gathas. "After Saoshy-ans comes they prepare the rising of the dead; as it says that Zartusht asked of Auharmazd thus: 'Whence does a bodily form come again; and how does the resurrection occur Compare the expression 'with what body do they come?']— And Auharmazd answered thus: 'When through me the sky arose from the substance of the ruby [it was supposed to be stony ***coela ruunt;*** cp. Y. XXVIII], and yet supported without columns, [see Y. XLIV, ***avapas toish***] on the spiritual support of far - compassed light [was fire also thought of?], — when through me the earth arose which bore the material life, and there is no maintainer of the worldly creation but it,—when by me the sun, moon, and stars are conducted in the firmament of luminous bodies;—when by me corn was created, so that, scattered about in the earth, it grew again and returned with increase; ['thou sowest not that body that shall be but naked grain'],—when by me color of various kinds was created in plants [flowers]; — when by me fire was created in plants [vegetable caloric] without combustion;— when by me a son was created and fashioned in the womb of a mother and the structure severally of the skin, nails, blood, feet, eyes, and ears and other things was produced.... each one of these, when created by me, was herein more difficult than causing the ***resurrection,*** for it is an assistance to me in the resurrection that they exist, [i. e., they exist actually on in their dissolution, resurrection being merely their re-construction]; but when they were formed it was not the forming of the future out of the past, [as the resurrection will be], and so it, the resurrection, will be less formidable as an undertaking than the original creation.

"When that which did not at all previously exist was then produced, at the creation (out of nothing) why is it not possible to produce again, [re-construct] that which was come in an existing body; for at that time, the time of the resurrection, one will demand the bone from the spirit of the earth, i. e., from the dust [recall Ezekiel 'bone to his bone/ also Daniel's 'rising from the dust] the blood from the water, the hair from the plants, and the life from the fire, since they were delivered to them in the original creation [at death]. First the bones of Gayomard [the Iranian Adam] are raised up ['the dead in Christ shall first arise'], then those of Mashyoi and Mashyoi, [the first human pair], then those of the rest of mankind. In the fifty-seven years of Soshyans, they prepare all the dead, and all men arise [stand up], whoever is righteous and whoever is wicked, every human creature ['I saw the dead, small and great, stand before God'];—they rouse them up from the spot where its life departs. Afterward when all material living beings assume again their bodies and forms, then they assign them each to a single class. Of the light accompanying the sun one-half shall be for Gayomard ['there is one glory of the sun'] of the stars ['Another glory of the stars'—'one star differs from another star in glory']; and one-half of the light will give enlightenment among the rest of men, so that the soul and body will know that is my father and this is my mother, etc,"

The Bundahesh is a very prominent work among the later Zoroastrian documents, and, as just implied, it postdates Christianity by some hundreds of years. But the expressions in Plutarch already alluded to, seem to indicate the prevalence of an almost exactly corresponding tone of thought as that of this later Zoroastrianism even as early as 100 to 300 B. C, and this strong eschatology is homogeneous in an unbroken chain with that of predecessors to the time of the Gathas, whereas the Jewish doctrine of the later days was an innovation of the time of the Exile intended to console the captives who had lost their homes and their property; see above. The same remark applies to all other post-Christian Zoroastrian doctrines.

CHAPTER VI.

THE JUDGMENT IN DANIEL AND IN THE EXILIC AND POST-EX-ILIC THEOLOGY IN GENERAL; SUBJEC-TIVE RECOMPENSE.

THE next most important particular which demands attention would be the Day of Judgment, or rather "a day of judgment"; for, as this feature occurs in Daniel, it was primarily judgment upon the Beast (see Dan. vii. 9-14) who had persecuted the saints see it supplemented by Revelations where the same original motive of vengeance is present, but where the act itself is represented as universal upon an assembled and risen mankind. So far as imagery is concerned, the Zoroastrian pales before its sequent, though Zoroastrianism shows a superior refinement and depth in one supreme particular; for not only does it concern itself more immediately and chiefly with the moral accountability and the future state than other systems of its date, but it offers the first well-certified occurrence of the great and crucial doctrine of Subjective Recompense, the idea that "virtue is its own reward, and vice its own punishment"; see below. Its awards were not exclusively of this character, and it might possibly be doubted whether the idea focussed itself in the thought that the fact of being "a sinner" was itself actually the doom and execution, or whether it first meant to suggest that the particular sins were in a way figuratively the personified executioners; but it is obvious that the one idea was not at all so very far distant from the other, and that the first was certainly foreshadowed in the last and that indeed it inevitably led on the mind at the next step to it. Subjective recompense was also not of course the whole of the Zoroastrian Heaven and Hell; but it was the soul of them,—and this might be said to be almost the crowning glory of this entire scheme, curious as such a statement may at first sight of it appear to some of us to be.

a. The Judgment in the Gatha.

In Y. XLIII, 4 we have: "For so I conceived of three as August [with others 'as Holy'], O Ahura Mazda, when I beheld Thee as supreme in the generation of life; when as rewarding deeds and words Thou didst establish evil for the evil, blest rewardings[45] for the good[46] by Thy just virtue[47] in the creation's final change. [48] (6) In which (last) changing Thou shalt come and with Thine August Spirit [others, 'and with Thy Holy Spirit'] and Thy Sovereign Power, O Ahura Mazda, by deeds of whom the settlements are furthered through the Righteous Order (of Thy Law) ; and (saving) regulations likewise unto these shall Ara-maiti offer [Angel of the ready will],—yea laws of Thine understanding which no man may deceive."[49] In another key of rhythm in the Gatha Ahunavaiti we have at Y. XXX, 4:

"Then those Spirits created as first they two come together life and our death decreeing, and how the world at

[45] hardly "riches" here.

[46] Notice the laws of judgment established from the foundations of the world, spoken of as if seen by reflective vision directed upon the original creation. Or are these preterits to be read in the sense of futures expressed in the sense of the improper conjunctive?

[47] I prefer the original meaning in this ancient passage—as expressing the "Justice" rather than the "wisdom" of God, for in the next verse "the omniscience" is given.

[48] "Revolution" is hardly the meaning here; "the turning" was an expression for "the end,"; see other passages.

[49] His judgment is infallible.

the last shall be (ordered). For the Evil (as Hell) the worst life, but for the Holy the Best Mental (state)...."

(8): "Then when Vengeance comes, Vengeance just upon the wretches...." (10) "There on the Host of the Druj the blow of destruction descendeth, but swiftest in the abode of the good Mind gather the righteous; with Mazda and Asha they dwell, advancing in their good fame."

Y. XXX, II : "When long is the wound of the wicked and blessings the lot of the saint."

Y. XXXI, 17: "And what debts are paid in justice for the offering of the Holy.— What is the wicked's debt, and their portion what in the Judgment?"

Y. XXXI, 21: "He who deceives the saint for him shall at last be destruction— long life in the darkness his lot, vile[50] his food, with revilings loathsome;—These be your world, O ye foul. By your deeds your own soul will bring it."

XLVI, 7: "Karps, yea, and Kavis are with foul kings joining, deeds which are evil with man's better life to slay;—cursed by their souls and selves, their being's nature, when from the Judgment's Bridge (they fall, the final pathway) ; —Ever in Demon's home—their bodies[51] lie."

XLIX, 11: "Then evil rulers, evildoers, evil speakers, those believing ill, and false men evil-minded, with evil food[52] the souls to meet are coming. In Druj's home at last their forms[53] (abide)" [or "in Falsehood's home at last the citizens(?)

(they are)"].

Y. LI: "He who than good better giveth, He who ren-

[50] Reproduced in the later Zoroaslrianism.

[51] More literally, "The K. and K. will join and with evil Kings, with evil rites and deeds, to slay the human life, whom (their) own souls and their own conscience will shriek at when they come where the Judgment Bridge (extends) ; for ever to all duration—their bodies, (lie) in the Druj's Abode."

[52] This is a fragment of the original of Yasht XXII.

[53] Or "as citizens (?) they are"; see above.

ders rewards for religion—is Ahura Mazda in His sovereign power; but He gives him worse than the evil—who does not impart offerings to Him—in the last end of the world."

Y. LI: "What satisfaction thou shalt give through Thy red flame, O Mazda, give as a sign[54] through the melted bronze [through the lake of fire] for both the worlds, [see verse 6] as an indication [or "implement"] for the wounding of the faithless and the prospering of the saint."

These may suffice as expressions from the old Avesta, the Gathas.

b. Judgment in the Later Avesta.

In the later Avesta at Vendidad XIX, we have: "O Maker of the material worlds, Thou Holy One, where are the awards given? Where does the rewarding take place? Where is the awarding fulfilled? Whither do men come for the reward which in their life in the material world they have made good for the soul ?"

Some of the more dramatic features of the supernatural judicial scene which appear in our Holy Scriptures are absent from the Avesta, or have perished from it; —yet this is again made up by the extraordinary subjectivity, which is present everywhere; for in answer to the above the soul seems to judge itself, justifying or condemning itself in the same manner as we have just seen in the Gathas, though this occurs on the sadder side of the matter, but even pleasing dramatic features intervene in this case in the later books Vendidad and Yasht XXII. For it, the soul (V. xix, 115) is met on the Chinvat Bridge, or at its entrance, by its own counterpart and is questioned by an image representing its conscience. A welcome which recalls the most touching passage in St. Matthew, (xxv.

[54] So I now think to be possible in view of the Bundahish; see above.

36-37),9 meets it. It then proceeds upon its path toward the summit of Hara Berezaiti, (HighMountain), the name still surviving in Elburz in the territory at the southwest corner of the Caspian till a late period.

There the soul comes before the golden throne of Vo-humanah, who strangely enough represents the "Holy Man" like the "Son of man" in the Gospels; see above;— and he, Vohumanah, is also indeed the Good Mind of God and of His saints personified, recalling our doctrine of the divinity of Christ, which represents Christ as being both God and man. He rises from his seat and greets the approaching saved man. One of the faithful beside Vohumanah, full of concern, asks him: "When didst thou come from that transitory world to this intransitory one? how long was they salvation?...."

The passage is of course a mass of fragments and we are left without his answer, though Ahura courteously intervenes with the remonstrance: "Ask him not of that cruel way...." The soul then passes on "contented," that is to say, beatified; "to the golden throne of Ahura Mazda —and to the golden thrones of the bountiful immortals, even to Garodmana, Heaven, the abode of sublimity or song, to the immortals and Ahura's home."

c. Judgment in the Later Zoroastrianism.

These delineations of Avesta are continued on the Bun-dahesh (say 500700 A. D.) and in other works of the later Zoroastrianism, with little or no diminution in the subjectivity of the described occurrences. In the Bunda-hesh on p. 122, we have: "Then is the assembly of Sad-vastar where all mankind will stand at this time."

In that assembly every one sees his own good deeds and his own evil deeds, and a wicked man becomes con-spicuous as a white sheep (sic!) among the black. After-wards they set the righteous man apart from the wicked, near and from afar" might indeed refer to the pilgrims for high - festival occasions doubtless referred to in Yasna XXX, i and XLV, i.

In either case, in both Gospel and Avesta, the soul is pleasingly bewildered, needing explanation as before: "When saw I thee a stranger?" in the Gospel; and in Avesta: "What is this fragrance?" and then, "What maiden art thou?"[55] and then here once again as if expostulating, 'Who hath desired thee hither?" or, as I should now render: "Who hath invited thee hither?"

"It is thus," she continues, [through thy good thoughts and words, and deeds, and by contenting the saint who came to thee from afar] "that thou hast made me who am lovely, still more lovely; I am beautiful and beatified; and thou hast made me still more beautiful and beatified; I am seated upon a higher seat, and thou hast made me still more exalted through thy good thoughts, and words, and deeds."— Totally aside from all possible and impossible literary connection, we certainly see in each case the same hesitating doubt with an affecting humility, and the same delighted satisfaction; and most singular of all from one of the same good deeds. It is from this on that the soul goes toward the golden thrones of Vohumanah, Ahura and the rest, as we saw above.

[55] So before, "What wind is this?"

CHAPTER VII.

ZOROASTRIANISM IN ITS DISTINCTIVE CHARACTERISTICS.

The More Precise Sense in which the Term is Applied Above.

IT may seem to some of my readers that this conclusion of my short treatise is hardly the place in which to clinch an important distinction as regards the chief one of all the subjects brought into consideration here. And this final and all-inclusive point or disc, is indeed the entire question of the definite aspect in which we have intended to view Zoroastrianism throughout, and this is especially contrasted with its two sister, or rather with its two closely related, systems, not exclusively so of course, but perhaps fundamentally so—most certainly so, to a very striking manner and degree.

But I have on the contrary the impression that, after having done all that lay within my power to do to awaken interest and to show how the intellectual forces which I proposed to marshal might be thought to tell upon the decision, it might then offer a sort of final incisive effect if I gather up the force of what has been said, and more closely define this one of the principal factors brought into operation. What then, in a distinctive or exclusive definition of it, is this particular Zoroastrianism, the partial effects of which I have endeavored somewhat closely to trace in my few pages above? And of course I mean by the inquiry to define its two sister systems which have been also necessarily brought to some degree into our view; for there exists, as might be expected, the most decided difference between the three, though "these varia-tions do not touch" the primal characteristics of all.

The Avesta and the Veda.

As to the Indian Veda, which is certainly the nearest relative of the Avesta on the southern or south-eastern side, I need hardly say that we have here no serious cause to linger further, as I have dwelt upon it elsewhere in fuller terms. The common elements of both Veda and Avesta involved in such a review of them as this, are familiar ; and they are also clear and definable;—but they were loosely scattered within the vast labyrinth of early lore which resembles rather an immense and florid forest, where the separated materials of both Avesta and Veda lay at hand, and from which both emerged, its home being far away from all contact with the southern land and up toward the north and north-west of Iran; while of the two the Avesta and Rig Veda, the Veda, let us concede it, far more closely resembles those original growths, (though so much more distant from the common original home) for the simple reason that there is more of it. A lore which is comparatively sparse, from that very fact cannot reproduce so many of the early features of its mother lore, as a sister branch can which is more voluminous. Veda, therefore, as a matter of course, shows more of the common original than Avesta. The Ameshaspends, chief concepts of Avesta, are there in the Veda as I have so fully shown in *Zara-thushtra and the Greeks,* but they were by no means present as a quintessence of selected and especially venerated significant ideas. They are there also totally unconscious of their kinship either with each other or with the selected six of the Avesta; in fact they are ordinary abstract thoughts personified at times indeed, but not distinctly grouped like those in Avesta, nor distinguished and exalted as they are in the Median lore, while one of them, and that one from the Iranian side, one of the most important, is merely the name of a late Vedic seer.

Outside of these few scattered concepts, noble and interesting as they must ever be, the differences as to the tone and substance are marked between the Avesta and the Rik. The highest gods of Veda seem to struggle in a throng to attain position above their colleagues; but this desired eminence is hardly the serious and solemn superiority occupied by the Iranian Ahura as he appears in the Avesta; nor does any one of them really arrive at such position as He seeks,—at least none of them reaches it to hold it;—southern imagination was too fervid, restless and creative. Southern life with its milder climates and swarming populations offered too wide an opportunity for both impassioned action, active conjecture, and vehement expression. Each great Deity has to defend his position against his on-coming rivals, one or more.

Zoroastrianism, that is to say, in its earlier form, that of the Gathas, is, on the contrary, almost our modern system, startling indeed beyond most other things, even when regarded solely as a literary curiosity, with its supreme and refined good Deity and with its excluded Devil—which last idea was indeed one of the best of great suggestions ever made to rid our God of all complicity with crime.

The vile thing, by this doctrine of an "independent Satan," is forever shut out from Him. Nowhere does the Veda show a trace of this; at least not definitely, while the Attributes are almost scattered as if lost amidst an interminable overgrowth;—so much for that relation with the Veda, so vitally essential as in its elements it is.

The Avesta and the Inscription.

But what of the Daric Inscriptions and their system, aside from what has been already said or implied above, where, as we see, the relation, so far as it at first presents itself, looks like identity out and out? And here I must pause to make a remark which is almost a stern reproach to science to be obliged to utter. It is that this question has never been put popularly into print and pressed home before, at least not in any effective and incisive way, though of course it must have been long since often loosely stated in scattered remarks and in many an essay.

As may be seen everywhere above, and in the larger work, the Daric Inscriptions are our great and only positive bridge of literary and historical connection between Israel and the Avesta; for they objectively form almost a constituent part of the Bible on the one side, and of the Avesta on the other; and perhaps of the two they stand closer to the early pre-Exilic Bible, curious as such a statement may at first sight appear to be. Surely no rational teacher of the Holy Scriptures can dwell on these striking Persian edicts in the Exilic Scriptures so vitally crucial as they are to all religious history, without at the same time eagerly scanning and deeply searching the Inscriptions of the very same imperial authorities on Behistan, Persepolis, etc. They possess, indeed, these last, and as of course, in common with the Avesta, that supreme feature, the presence of a God as the Creator of heaven and earth, so termed with a predominant iteration, and therefore they are conspicuously marked above all other documents of their kind ancient or modern. He, Auramazda, is upon those Inscriptions a Supreme Good Being whose memorable name was identical in very form with the Supreme God of the Avesta; and this gives us what most of all we need when we compare the terms of the two lores, the Daric and the Iranian. Taken together with the devotional fervor of Darius expressed, as none such religious aspirations have ever been, in his ever repeated appeals and ascriptions of thankful adoration, these particulars constitute one of the most effective conjunctions of intellectual circumstances of their kind and nature ever recorded or pointed out;—but it is also of course to the last degree necessary to show the limits of these signal advantages in the comparison;—and here we have to lay down a principle which is strictly critical and unsparing. It is this: while it is in the first place certainly true beyond all reasonable question that there existed both a knowledge of the Avesta as a series of Medic documents, and also of its general main features on the part of the persons who dictated the texts from which the stone-cutters chiseled the Inscriptions of Behistan, etc., we are, nevertheless, forced to study our sculptured texts in those Inscriptions themselves and in them chiefly, if not in them alone, in order to find out what the creed of their composer was; for unless we positively assume that the now surviving Avesta furnishes the immediate background to the ideas expressed in the Inscriptions, then aside from those Inscriptions themselves, meagre as they must of necessity have been, we possess no such record of the detailed opinions of those authors, Darius and his successors, at all. While, indeed, taking into consideration the necessarily limited extent of the Inscriptions as literary matter, they might be regarded in some aspects of them as being almost the most prominent signal documents of all Monotheism, Creation-ism and of passionate personal devotion at their date, yet, for all that, they are by no means at all so near the Israelitish creed in the point of their doctrines as the Avesta is; and we cannot leave our subject until we make this clear.

The Dualism.

Strange as it may seem, we cannot even affirm from these majestic memorials alone (i. e., from the Texts of Behistan, etc.), that the priests of Darius actually held even to the more closely defined dualism of the Avesta, though they unquestionably held to the chief female demon who appears in it, and I believe that she or he, for the demon might be male(?) in the Inscriptions, has in the Daric creed, as in Avesta, a **Master**, for such systems are generally **pyramidal** ; and that this Master corresponded to the Angra Mainyu of Avesta seems to be probable in the extreme; and if this was the case, then it was practically certain that he was one of the Two Original spirits; as he is so definitely stated to be in the North Persian writings. He may indeed not have been called by the full title "Angra Mainyu" in the lore of the Inscriptions, but by some modification of it. Or, again, he may have lost in the Achæ-menian lore that independence of Auramazda which is of such vital moment in Avesta, just as under the form of Satan he lost it later in the Gospels, where he is completely (?) under the power of the Almighty, and this while he may have retained the name in full or modified.

Each of these possibilities, and any others that can be reasonably presented, must be taken into consideration by us, for such a question as this of the Dualism is, even when regarded as a side-issue, of the utmost interest as well as of the gravest importance as an intellectual religious circumstance; and in our serious endeavors to exploit the entire matter, we should here proceed with the utmost care and circumspection, with regard to it; for we should regard it as a positive certainty that there existed a mass of religious lore in Persia proper which has now been lost to us;—all surviving allusions to Mazda-worship in Greek and Latin authors seeming to refer to the Medic or Zoroastrian form of it.

The Ameshaspends.

Nor can we say with certainty that those composers of the Inscriptions accepted the Ameshaspends; see above, though it is practically certain that they heard their names re-echoed on every side;[56] nor does the word "Deva" occur upon the Inscriptions; so that my readers must understand that, in bringing in the above Mazda-worship, I refer distinctly to the Avesta for my main points as to the detail of the Persian and Exilic eschatology, and not at all immediately to the Inscriptions in my main arguments, for it is in the Avesta, and in that alone, with its implied predecessors, that we have the acme of analogy with the Exilic Judaism. Nothing of its kind approaches it in this respect in the history of any religion with which I am acquainted, unless in cases where the one religion has been distinctly a descendant of the other; that is to say, nothing that is prominent and well assured. Avesta and the Exilic Bible should be to all conscientious searchers the question of the hour. So much for this.

What is Exilic?

But another matter indeed of an analogous character presses closely upon us with the implied demand to make it finally plain in the full scope of all our inferences.

We have been talking at every juncture of what is Exilic, pre-Exilic, and post-Exilic. But what do we really mean by it all? What is then really "Exilic" in a closer definition? The distinction is of course the one most vital of its kind of all that one can possibly make with regard to the Bible; and I have indeed necessarily foreshadowed everywhere what I am now about more distinctly and more

[56] See my Zarathushtra, the Achæmenids, and Israel, at the places as per index.

fully to repeat, as it will be nearly essential for me to clinch what I have already said above by putting it in the clearest light and emphasis; for, like the other distinctions just made, it is seldom so pointedly presented as it ought to be in its full argumentative force.

Exilic and Pre-Exilic.

The matter in its closer point is this: We everywhere speak of the "Exilic Books"; but it is an obvious and pressing fact that much Exilic matter is present in many places in our at present so-called pre-Exilic texts; we might indeed be imperatively forced to doubt the uninfluenced existence of any pre-Exilic texts at all, for how could that primeval lore have been preserved intact; since all knowledge of important parts of it was even entirely lost in such a period as the reign of Josiah.[57] And in a discussion like this, Exilic matter, if it exists even at all in the Books which we have hitherto called pre-Exilic, becomes, if recognized, equally with the peculiar doctrinal elements of the later books, an almost supremely dominant factor.

What then are the particulars which thus control to a wide extent the situation here?

Perils of the Manuscripts.

It would be like trifling with it for us to ask whether any persons of credit anywhere suppose that the Hebrew Bible has been miraculously preserved, or preserved otherwise than in the usual manner, according to the regular laws of nature. We may therefore take it at once for granted that all serious readers here believe that the texts of the Old Testament and New Testament have been handed down to us in manuscripts—like all other ancient documents of their kind,—and it is indeed a circumstance marvelous enough that they, or any other ancient docu-

---

[57] Kings xxii. 8. See the impression produced by the finding of the Book of the Law in the Temple even in that enlightened reign.

---

ment at all, have been handed down to us in any form; for the continuous life of ancient books before the art of printing is indeed as strange a phenomenon as the re-appearance of plants or animals in separated continents divided by water from the rest of the world. So, even of our Holy Scriptures, one would suppose that a single breath of war or political agitation would literally shake what is preserved in brittle manuscripts almost to irrecoverable fragments; and undoubtedly every convulsion, such as a campaign or an exilic deportation, has diminished the volume of these precious objects which have however lived on in their mysterious pertinacity. Schools of copyists existed everywhere, of course, as well as individual skilled penmen. The scribes were obviously closely occupied in every center of religious learning as an essential element, and some of them in every detached community must have been charged with the especial care of the sacred rolls. And if this were the case while the Temple still stood, how much more must it have been the case in the keen religious revivals of the Exile? Then, as we have already seen, the avalanche of sorrows which first stupified, then infuriated, and at last reformed the holy race, made them search all the more solemnly their religious scriptures.

The to them, doubtless, most impressive pageants of their ritual had exercised unquestionably much restraining influence of a favorable character upon their minds as well as stimulated to some degree the active elements in their faith, and in fact it had been all-important in consolidating and preserving their intense unity as a people; —but temporal and corporeal considerations held their sway, as was most natural, in the incessant struggle and friction of their doubtless busy national and civic life in its periods of prosperity,—with all its fervent passion and its vivid color:—and this may be readily seen in the marvelous literary productions of the Exilic period. But the war of the Exile came,—and their existence as a nation was terminated or suspended. At first their experiences were bitter indeed, with the effect that their beautiful lyrics were the more often heard stirring the calm evening air in the rural suburbs of Babylon and in its surrounding provinces. The songs of Zion become then their consolation,—and since the sacred scenes of the Temple no longer survived to impart support to them, they began all the more eagerly to read and search their to them inspired scriptures;—yes, and to write further such compositions for themselves so that to those bards of the "sad" Captivity we owe most of the sublimer passages of all the Semitic Revelation. Then surely they redoubled every effort to preserve and multiply the surviving documents of their Holy Law, written doubtless upon skins, which would bear the wear and tear of constant use better than the later materials, if indeed any other materials were ever really known to them.

Recopying of course took place, as it had never been so pushed on before; and it was done by men who lived near Babylon among the Persian garrisons as well as im-mediately within the "Cities of the Medes." Do we suppose that those tribes so forcibly settled in these "Cities," which must have been to some degree of it important centers, were of all conceivable Jewish communities the only ones without their Rabbis, their ordinary priests, their scribes and their Exile-archs? Here then was Judaism in the heart of Media which was even more Zoroastrian than Persia proper or than Persian Babylonia. Was notRagha itself a chief one of those very "Cities of the Medes" to which allusion is twice made categorically in Kings;— Ragha which was a very hot-bed of Zoroastrianism? Surely Ragha, as almost the center of the tale of Tobit, has high claims to have been at least one of those places where the tribes were originally placed. Among the literary people of those tribes was many a one who had at least some admission to the circles of the great satraps, while as to those who had settled near Babylon, the kings themselves lived hard by at the summer palace city, Shushan, amidst the breezy hills of Elam, and both military and royal processions must have often occupied the roads. These imperial people, as we see from Ezra and his successors, knew much of the "Great God" of their new subjects; and that the Jewish leaders knew something of their faith, in reciprocating interest, it would be ridiculous to doubt; information on the one side here of course presupposes information on the other. *Avidity* is none too strong an expression to describe the curiosity with which the gifted Semites must have questioned every Persian priest among their other new found fellow citizens, though in the case of the Babylonians the first ferocities of resentment must be allowed time to have worn away.

"What was then, more precisely, this religion of their great deliverer with its God so like their own Yahveh? And what were these angelic beings whose names were echoed everywhere among their new-found friends?"— for they were later the very names of the months and days among these North Medic officers, and they may well have been so then ;[58]—and beside this with little doubt the beings whom they designated were even worshiped constantly at various divisions of the day. If then they could really understand that these noble words meant in their first application more, far more, than the titles of mere angels,— that they were actually the descriptive appellations of God's attributes; see above, and only then later personified as His first creatures,—how striking this must have appeared to them. And—what was this deep doctrine "as to thought, as to word, and as to deed"? How melodious too were those Gathic chants in meters sister to the Veda

[58] See above.

which they now for the first time heard;—and how strange this doctrine of a resurrection,—of an advanced Heaven and Hell,—of millennial hopes, etc. Surely it is impossible that the Jewish schools of Babylon, not to speak again of those in the "Cities of the Medes," should not have known something about the faith of their Persian king, whose troops and courtiers, and beyond all question whose priests also, swarmed on every side with the usual staffs of assisting acolytes. Ignorance here seems simply inconceivable. They must have been little indeed like their successors, the well-known Jewish seers of keenest wit in Babylon, if they knew nothing of all this. Unlike indeed the men who founded the impressive schools at that great center, and who wrote our Exilic Bible for us, with our finest Talmud;—little of their kind indeed were they, if they did not find out all that Cyrus's priests could tell them, while the great King was doubtless himself seen often in his first Capitol both in ordinary imperial resi-dence and in the ever-intervening crises of his reign. Remember how closely even an Alexander some centuries later on could question the Persian Destoors as to their lore with its impressive creed—while at later than the latter's date Jewish stories were half pure Persian in Medish scenes; see above.

" Every Exile prophet, whose works have survived to us, shows that he breathed a new-found atmosphere; though he may have learned the Persian tenets by hearsay only and at second or indeed only at third hand, just as they must have later heard of the great inscriptions when they were newly cut and of many a predecessor of them now long since vanished, for that their replicas were everywhere is clear from Behistan. Those on that rock could not be at all reached by the passing wayfarers who might wish to read. Copies therefore of their substance, if not0020of their letter, must have been provided, and they must have been amply in evidence in every higher school.

The contrary to this is excluded absolutely from all sane consideration; see also the alleged messages from Cyrus on his side as also those from Darius, Xerxes, and Artaxerxes; and see their edicts in our Bibles with the throngs of ordinary Persian words and names like Mithra-dates, among those of the Jews. These things do not prove intercourse; they are "intercourse" itself. And as the prophets, so the priests, and the priestly scribes; the devoted men toiled doubly for many a weary day copying and recopying the holy texts. That they did not restore, interpolate and emend them everywhere is inconceivable, if for no other reason, then because they were often for the most part quite half the time half-legible; and duty itself would call on them to bring the dim tracings back; whole folios and even masses of folios would be also lost, gone doubtless forever. Emendations were therefore made everywhere at frequent intervals; see above; could this have been avoided? And this took place, as we must clearly see, all the more with regard to the oldest and most sacred parts of Holy Writ. Do we suppose that the skins on which Genesis was painted were really any stronger than those inscribed with the first Isaiah, or that the pigments used as ink were less capable of effecting corrosions in the course of time? Often indeed would the oldest scripture stand recopied in the newest handwriting and upon the freshest scroll. Their new-found ardor, born of their adversities and their new associations, had created the searching diatribes of Ezekiel and of the rest,— and it is inconceivable that the re-writers did not add stirring passages even in the oldest documents to their studies in their endeavor to restore and point the meaning here and there. Little indeed of the Holy Scriptures of those early dates has been left at all to us, comparatively speaking, precious beyond measure as that little is,[59] and everywhere throughout the documents which were preserved fresh and live thoughts have been implanted as the needs arose. And from this let us gather our ideas of the "Exilic" elements in the former still embedded in the Semitic books throughout the very oldest documents, though of course these very emendations have themselves shared somewhat the fate of their primeval predecessors. Time and accident, travel, exile, war and sacrilege have of course changed text after text, and this beyond all question even in the oldest books.

Yet what is original is not so hard to recognize; simply because the Exilic inter-polations are so clear. I will not prolong this point;—this conclusion is but intended to be a short remark. Everywhere throughout the oldest books of the pre-Exilic Bibles, the re-writers inserted their keener thoughts: so that "pre-Exilic" is a very dubious term. We must search the very texts of the Hexateuch for it if we would do our work, for Exilic matter must be everywhere.

With this I close my brief essay, begun at the request of a distinguished friend, but here expanded far beyond the limits of a short Appendix, all that was at first in-tended.

For a still greater substitute more hastily struck off, see Appendix IV of the able conservative work of the Rev. C H. H. Wright on Daniel, Vol. II, 1906.

[59] It would be indeed almost a miracle, if truth can assure us that one tenth of our earliest Bible has actually survived, holy and sacrosanct as that fragment so truly is,—emendation, interpolation, excision went on everywhere *part passu* with defacement, corrosion, theft, burning, vandalism, and every loss. Exilic matter crops out everywhere throughout.

CHAPTER VIII.

GOD AND HIS IMMORTALS.

Ahura.

AHURA, the life-Spirit-Lord, existed as a word in its form of Asura from im-memorial ages in the common primeval home of Veda and Avesta; and no name could be nobler for a holy God. It is better than Deus,—Zeus, which referred to the shining sky; better than "God," far ***better*** in its origin at least; for, curiously enough, it expresses the same supervening ideas that we have in the Hebrew Yahveh which was later thought to mean "the being One," the "I am that I am."[60] This is the very same concept which lives essentially and etymologically in Ahura; for He is the source and interior of being, *Ahura* ; and, so far as I can remember, this is the deepest epithet that has ever been prominently applied to Deity. With this we have the other name Mazda, "the Great Creater," or with tradition the "Great Wise One." No words could be more impressive nor more interpenetrating.[61]

The Amesha Spenta.

While the six characteristics—virtues would not be the proper word—are absolutely the main laws of a righteous universe, clear and pure. Simple indeed they are, as all things universal must be;—common too, as the breath-

[60] An unquestionably later interpolation of Exilic origin.

[61] Nor have any more impressively effective appeared in history.

air that we breathe, for life is common; they are the most interior and elevating forces in all that we really know, or so to us they should be. Here they are in a sense collected; and in them all that is fittest for expression speaks to us. Not of themselves only do they thus impel us, once merely uttered, and then left wandering, scattered as it were amidst an innumerable host of other similarly treasured spiritual things. Gems of imperishable cost they would be, or they are, even then as so dispersed, and so existing to us, though almost irretrievably hidden amidst the throngs of other beauty from our most eager sight. And so indeed they actually once lay strewn like jewels of first water all dull and unpolished and rarely recognized in the bed-rock of their unwrought mines or buried in their native clay;—vague surmises were they ever even then of the eternal way in which the beneficial powers sometimes work for us for good. But here, as seen, they are gathered up for us; not like the glittering objects in a diadem,—that would be *indeed* too low an image,—not like the flowers upon a full-flushed tree, but like the solar systems around their central orb. Like this these all-pervading order-forces revolve around the throne of their Great Sovereign;—nay more, they actuate the very Person of the God Omnipotent,—in honor—they are not His decorations ; far from it,—God forbid. They are His very Nature. He is the self-dividing, all enclosing Prism of them all,—the One of glorious hues that fold and unfold themselves in everlasting light. They are in a word God's character, than which no further thought is thinkable. And as the eternal ideals of all truth and order, they are those essential conditions of well-being, toward which all sentient subjects spiritually gravitate and should forever yearn;—and they are here enthroned,—made dominant,— set over everything in a way pre-eminent, though they have indeed evolved themselves through long preceding ages, nay rather, though they have gathered crystal-like in their clusters through previous cycling aeons.

Asha.

Asha, the very first law of all our better consciousness, here even seriously gains in its application, marvelous as such a thing may seem to some of us to be.

It, Asha, is indeed itself and in itself, Heaven's and nature's first moral guide, here declared also to be the first principle of God's eternal being. It is lifted up by all that there is in the conception of the divine personality,— brought into operation,— becoming at once when established among the Six a mighty challenging idea flinging its defiance at that one gigantic, but malign element, its opposite, the Lie, a spirit demon which withers us on every side. It proclaimed the Truth in the post-ultimate meaning of the word, asserting that there was indeed such a thing as a law actual,— and this not as a pointless sentiment, feebly fluttering, but as the very first instinct of God's character. From eternity past it has been the same, so in the vital present, and to all coming futurity will it abide unchangeable.

If we, who struggle to maintain honor, believe God to be indeed a person, here is a support immeasurable for us. The great crucified but risen Christ of faith cheers all our efforts on, for it has an almighty mind to harbor it and to guard it, to assist it, and proclaim it in the very ultimate essence of its worth;—for of such a mind is it indeed an all-controlling, dominant, though merely regulative part.

What a consolation indeed for those who think Truth possible and who believe in God in any sense of Him;—to think that there is at least one person who is True,—and *such a Person!* And we see how beautifully such a creed applies itself. Here we have a God omnipotent to protect us, and to further us, and to bless us;—but He consists, in part at least, of fidelity; and we have no connection with Him save as we are faithful. Abandon honor and He vanishes. There is no God but the *true God, the Asha-God.*

But like all things of its nature the growth of this great but simple principle, in its recognition of course I mean, was, as I say, but gradual.

It developed at first slowly enough indeed, as we may both most readily conjecture and concede, with languid signs of life as its first glimmer shone among the vague dreams of sentient beings, glowing feebly into fuller light And elsewhere and aside from either, it seems to have been in fact the very last and most remote of all the ideas to be recognized as concentered and so elevated in the forms of ancient creeds, as at all in any way a particular trait of any one of all the beings called "divine," not even of the chief of them, so luxuriantly depicted as they are in the wreaths of our immortal song.

Even in the pre-Gathic age it, Asha of the Holy Truth, was of course surmised dimly as a universal regulative power;—but only by degrees did it unfold itself into clear consciousness as it grew, as all things like it must. That is to say, the very first idea of it as a concept developed but tardily as our race rose from its animal predecessors. —Some sort of consecutive sequence may indeed have even revealed itself to the instincts of the higher animals; the next beneath us; but it is better to confine ourselves to man.

The observed regularity in the sequence of natural phe-nomena first riveted attention as we grew human;—especially the heavenly bodies seemed to follow some rule, chief of all and naturally the God-like sun, which was often seen quite unclouded for long periods in lands called Iran. Its august reappearances followed

Law even in its supervening changes in situation and intensity, with occasional eclipse. It never failed, and on its fidelity the balance of all existing necessary objects seemed to hang. Without one phase of it planting would be impossible, without another harvest, without a third the source of tonic health.

Soon the moon, its brother luminary, for the moon is masculine both in Veda and Avesta, took up the tale with his five changes, and with these the reverting atmospheric modifications seemed to harmonize.

The main features of the advancing year-time seemed ever calculable. The great wind-storms of the Marutis, with their driven clouds flying on before them, seemed to arrive at certain intervals in many regions including India, with the return of ice and snow elsewhere and mostly hated,—the periodic rains torrential or soft and fertilizing, the dews and the flowering earth itself:—these all followed one another at seeming regulated intervals;—it was Asha, order. Endeared among all else was the inextinguishable fire not only blazing in the ever self-consuming God of day, but in the very bowels of the earth, known too in the caloric of plants, flaming also in forked lightning in the heavens, snake-like in figure;—again it was the friend of man on hearth and altar. Asha became its very synonym, and so from this its sacredness, from regularity; it was indeed "God's son."[62] Then too the great ocean tides, to recall again the waters, with their ever measurable ebb and flood, could not have been altogether unknown to them, our early forebears, through hearsay, though living inland: —so too the spring freshets with swollen streams were ever to be looked for in their times. All was the unvarying circling forms of recurring certainty;—it was Asha, *rita,* "rhythm." It reigned supreme in the terrific as in the genial.

What wonder then that they began to think that the thoughts of God were similar, supposing always that they had at that time any distinct idea whatsoever of a God,—

[62] A frequent expression as applied to it in the late Avesta.

that His law in some of its interior elements would harmonize with this rhythm "as to thought, as to word, and as to deed";—that is to say, that it should be "perfect, converting the soul."

All was symmetric in its movements; that is, all was Asha. It was "nature" always and everywhere, *natura,* "to be born," and to be born again, *natura,* not *futura* merely, but natura, to be rhythmically born in a reappearance never unreasoned in its process, — seed, stem, leaves, fruit, to seed, stem, leaves and fruit again,— stream, mist, cloud, rain, to stream, mist, cloud, rain again,— spring freshness, summer bloom, autumn harvest, winter frost with cheer or misery, to spring, bloom, harvest, frost again. It was law forever fulfilling itself,—Asha, Rita, Rhythm.

So in the old Veda, in those early days, when man had however somewhat begun to form himself; Rita was so distinctly recognized that the very ceremonial service to the Heavenly Spirits followed its course in imitation. "Rite" appeared as Rita; that is to say, regularity in disciplined religious action in a form spectacular, presented ceaselessly and seldom varying, never abruptly, strictly and strenuously carried out by priests with closest care, consecrated for the ceremonial in sacrifice and praise.

But it was only in the stern Gatha, rough and sparse but glorious, that the Rita, Asha, became so exalted as the passionate honor of an Holy God in a sense supreme, a deity whose creature, the very foremost of all the other divine beings it was declared to be.[63] What an exaltation, let me again assert it, for simple but awful justice, the first pure principle of all sane consciousness at least in man, and as we see, the first spiritual force in God. He is not an "infinite person," which could only be the language of

[63] Mithra, a noble God indeed like the most exalted of our Archangels, whose cult rivaled Christianity for a long time.

inadvertence, for a "person cannot be infinite,"[64] but He is a *universal person* in whom we live and move; the Great Omnipotent, Omniscient, All-holy;—

and He is *ashavan,* no liar.

Vohu Manah.

Then Vohu Manah, the "Good Mind," was again a thing enthroned, and for that alone, if for nothing else, made eminent. This was again too a curious thought in a savage age in far off Persia to be placed in such position —for then it was that the gods of Greece wrangled like vulgar households and even our Jewish Yahveh was a "consuming fire."

Vohu Manah;—it was a deep yearning in the universe toward all the good, making what was best in their sentient longings real. It was more than a tame ne-gation, a lifeless acquiescence; it was a warm breath of active sympathy, a passion pervading conscious nature everywhere like a befriending instinct, a slender thread of sweetness in all the intricacies of interior feeling that gives us hope through the maniac jars of this thing which we call life. Vohu Manah;—it was all that is holiest in emotions, fervor in pure breasts and brains; the quiet force in the love of man for his brother; the power in the noble love of man for woman so deep and so trans-forming, fierce too also at times, past holding;—Vohu Manah—it is the father's solemn all-giving watchfulness which makes the name of "son" our deepest word.

Above all else it is the mother-love, that nerve of all controlling tenderness planted in every female soul over a little thing endowed for that very reason with a charm unspeakable,—to win and keep. And this Vohu Manah is again not left,— according to the Gatha,—a blind, un-guided force, though beatific, in the world of sentient be-

[64] Definition implies limit; see below.

ing;—it is an attribute and emotion of a Supreme Person (morally supreme)— Vohu Manah,—it meant the deep love of Almighty God for all the righteous living under His holy eye;—His creatures all the good were, and so was, in a still nearer sense, each one of them His child.

Khshathra.

With Khshathra we come upon the deeply fundamental element of **Rule.**

Not men, nor angels can persist without it. Some forceful form of right is needed to control and maintain the Law and Love, shaping their every application

Khshathra, government, administration!—without it chaos would ensue. With anarchy all property would turn worthless; no man could earn his bread; progress would be imperilled. Khshathra is command, severe indeed at times. Strength must emerge from commonplace while commonplace resists it. Conspiracy is unveiled by government—law put in force, Khshathra as "strength" meant discipline, combination with organization;—without it rallying points would be difficult, and the du-sh-Khshathra would sweep the isolated hordes away. Fields could not be cultivated save from Aeshma, "Raid fury of the bloody spear." And Khshathra rules in fact in every sentient being from the mammoths to the ant-tribes, while man is paramount because of it. And what a satisfaction have we here again, who believe the Gatha. Khshathra is not alone a universal law—though marvelous indeed as such he would be, or he is—part of the moving crystallization of the ever re-forming universe; the forceful way in which things come and hold together, while like the flying blood they circulate. It is more: it is the *rule of our Sovereign God over us.* Where would be, indeed, the Truth—instinct of sincerity though it is? where the Love, to lead us on, if there be no actual accordant *Power* ? In Gatha it is *the authority of God* , as universal Monarch, exercising His might throughout His all-world and at every pulse.

We at times indeed lose courage, recalling our human administrations;—but if we believe that *God is King,* our hopes revive. According to the divine doctrine, and in the full implications, every needed office in every government, as well as every official, was and is in the very fact energized and vivified by Khshathra as the controlling force in the Life-spirit-Lord. He stands through Khshathra in every court of justice seeing that the wronged are protected. With his Khshathra he controls the voice of evidence, the judge's faith. He is present in the arm of execution, bars the prison gates, and strikes the oppressor dead. In the wide conflicts of politics He is above all things dominant, as Khshathra. In war He orders the compact mass through it;—straightens the flagging lines. It is His Khshathra that brings on ***verethraghna,*** victory, saving an imperiled land;—and in the result His authority supports the well-won, or the long established, throne. God is everywhere supreme according to the doctrine, always as implied[65]—through this authority; without His firm grasp all rules would be reversed.

Aramaiti.

And then there was the Aramaiti, the Toil-Mind, the ara-thought of God; vivification of the holy, sacred forces just depicted, the self-movement throughout all better things; motion perpetual,—the eternal nerve indeed of holiness never for an instant left relaxed.

The Ara-mind of the Truth and Love and Power,— first stirring the ploughshare in the mould,—to ar in ara-

> [65] Here I treat once for all the mental forces implied everywhere;— seldom are these things actually expressed in Avesta as to their preciser point;—but everywhere ***implied*** in every line.

trum, —making fair life possible, displacing murder, theft and arson.

It was in fact in the first keen idea of it, ***holy work,***— and above all that of husbandry, first deed of virtue; the very earth itself from this took on the name in both Veda and Avesta. With it she also is Aaramaiti, and as such sacred. Aramaiti should be to us the point of everything, the practical application of the other noble three. It was the central open secret of all the Gathic existence; and it was vital. It was the life, virile thought of effort as against lazy theft. It found the tribes swept by the murderous raids of ferocious neighbors drunk with greed, their homes destroyed, their crops devastated, and their holy herds driven off, by Aeshma. Retaliation threatened to turn them too to murder; but the Gathic voice arose, as ever fresh, calling for civilization with honest toil. The armed saint of the Gathic battle was the *fshushyant* par eminence as against the *afshushyant,* —this distinctly.

He was "the cattle-breeding husbandman" toiling in the field with ara-thought, as against Aeshma. Where was the use of the Law, the Love, the Authority with hordes of starving families on land abandoned, derelict,— with savage bands rushing often headlong in, filling their barns with the plundered crops and raided flocks of murdered husbandmen?

How could the Law prevail without something in which the Law could have its existence,—a nation. Ara-maiti in one keen sense of it, and at its first idea was "industry," as I insist—without it no householder could accumulate the very means of civil life; for it is the persistent, wise, practical and so accumulating citizen, who builds up his country, as we know. Blustering disturbers, even when half well-meaning, waste the bread. The first duty of a human creature is to earn its living; if it does not

[66] This is my suggestion.

do that, it eats some other being's food, makes others poorer, is the cause of famine.

Enough has been said to make my idea clear. It was energetic occupation and first of all for the one thing needful, bread, honest bread for the hungry, tilling the Holy Earth, herself the sacred Aramaiti.[67] This was the idea's origin, as I think; and it was a worthy and noble one, becoming soon exalted even in that far-off day till it took its place upon the very brow of Deity among the Creator's attributes. Here too it gave the keynote to the rest.

As it was the sacred instinct of mind-directed labor settling the destiny of man toward manhood, stopping his tendency to remain a beast of prey; so it became zeal, the "zeal of the Lord of hosts" in other cycles of idea—spontaneous instigation, instinctive planned activity. It was the main-spring of the never erring mechanism, driving on the mother-love with ever-living thrills of tenderness, moving on forever keen and fresh the father's active thoughtfulness. It impelled the fire of mind in the expressed emotions of the singer and composer;—filled out the organizer's schemes, kept up the ardor of the scholar keen and rapid and maintained it discovering, advancing. It was the quickness of the soldier, combining movements at a glance, —the genius of invention, building out the world's capacities. It was the *ara-maiti,* self-toiling thought, stirring the hand and ear of creative passion everywhere. It was, in a word, our *Inspiration.*

In God, the divine instinct of activity, the essential force in spirit-motion; in man inspired obedience, in woman, piety, mild indeed, half unconscious, but still strenuous through all. No wonder that in pleasing memory God called it "daughter." It is the burning soul of the

[67] So too in Veda.

other three, the friend of Truth, the sister of Mercy, the handmaid of Command.

Haurvatat.

Haurvatat was the completeness of it all, again made here magnificent. She was the realization of the ideal, the wealth of health, and the health of wealth, in fact that very vision of perfection that should float as an ideal on the surface, or above every optimistic scheme to help it on and to make it actual. It was, in a word, *Fruition.* Who has not tasted somewhat of it at fleeting moments? It meant that justice should be more than a delusive subterfuge, hiding the sinister approach of theft forever creeping towards us. It meant that Love's longings should sometime touch their dearest goal, that just power should really reach dominion, that all nature's good instincts should succeed. It was with another's word, "to be satisfied." The name itself means All-ness, Haurvatat, the Vedic *sarvatat,* the great wall of full attainment enclosing the other Four. And goal and aim of all we hope for, we have again the satisfaction of it **This Allness is again of God:** and if He be the Haurva, sarva, All, surely there is some expectation left to us that we may one day gain what our better instincts wish.

Ameretatat.

While Immortality, as ever lifted up in Attribute, should be the permanence. God has no beginning, and so we all shrink with Him from an ending. Death is to some of us, delusively, woe's ultimate. One can scarce refrain from citing the schooldays' rhymes so beautiful, though sad, of Halleck:

"Come to the bridal chamber, Death!
Come to the mother's, when she feels
For the first time her first-born's breath!
Come when the blessed seals
That close the pestilence are broke,
And crowded cities wail its stroke!
Come in consumption's ghastly form,
The earthquake shock, the ocean storm !
Come when the heart beats high and warm,
With banquet song, and dance, and wine!
And thou art terrible!—the tear,
The groan, the knell, the pall, the bier,
And all we know or dream or fear
Of agony are thine."

But the holy faith held out its banishment. The glory of the Truth, the deep satisfaction of the Love, the sense of safety from the Power, the Inspiration and the Fruition should not end in inanition. The cup was not to be put to the lip only to excite desire, and to be dashed from it. There was to be an Ameretatat—death-absence. Like the Aditi of the Veda, Ahura was without beginning of days, and so consequently without end of years:—Eternity, Oh Eternity !—this, in another sense. As there was no beginning in God, so there was never a beginning to His works. He had put them forth from past eternity, and He will continue to do the like on to endless futurity, the same;—and so the life of the holy man should be deathless to a degree even here; but it should be also supernaturally immortal;—and this, when pointed, awoke everywhere the deepest hope, "bringing life and immortality to light." Strange as it may seem to us, the other life came largely from Arya, from Iran, from India. Veda with Avesta first pointed its significance. The Semites could at first see little reason in it. The great doctrine however is the vital force of Christianity, and the habitable world, so far as it is Christian, has lived on it for nineteen hundred years. Such are the immortals of the Gatha in their ideas expanded, well-called the "august," as they are. This only, be it noticed, is their meaning in the first keen conception of them in the first department of the Gatha;—and they are as I need hardly linger to re-asseverate, the sublimest conceptions of their particular kind that the world had till then ever seen,[68] for here they were signally assembled for us,—and doubly re-consecrated, as the essence of all holiness in a pure God personified.

Their Counterparts.

But the Opposer intervenes;—for, as against the supreme Life-Spirit-Lord, with His six characteristics, and in the pervading antithesis of the system the great Antagonistic Being, Angra Mainyu,[69] the Evil Spirit, appears, and stands in great prominence as perhaps the most defined concept of the kind ever advanced in all well-known theology. He is the Creator of all that is averse to the Good.

His attributes are not as yet at all so closely summar-ized in the Gathas as those of Ahura are, nor are they indeed formally collected even in the later but still genuine Avesta. They are however yet both implicitly and explicitly present in the Gatha as in the later Avesta, and with incisive force throughout.

Asha, the holy rhythm of fidelity in God and nature, first[70] of the sacred and august six Attributes just above discussed, [71] is met at every turn by its contradictory opposite, manifested, as might be expected, in the sinister shifts of subterfuge.

[68] In such remarks I refer, as I always try to make it plain, to well certified written lores.

[69] Literally the "Torturing Spirit" from the idea of "tortion," but the literal ideas of etymology are seldom to be followed closely in defining the particular meanings of a word. Simply "evil" is the sense.

[70] So in the original documents,—the Gathas; Asha leads us to its interior force and meaning. Not so later; Vohu Manah gained the prior place, doubtless, from its pleasing-significance.

[71] See above.

Jealousy, that first recognized of all the loathsome instincts in Bible, Veda, Iliad, and our Avesta, sheds its green gleam over the form of truthful innocence with the natural results at once apparent, the young, like Abel, in their first truthfulness are everywhere betrayed.

Suspicion, alas too often justified, is sown throughout. Treachery, as we even see it now, more and more pervaded intercourse, till Ferocity abode its time.

Murder was the mere outspoken expression of it all, led off, as might be expected, by the offspring of the first human pair (see Genesis); or later on in a finer garb as wreathed in the glare of a madman's joy it appeared in the hour of long planned infamy, the assassin gloating over his victim. Every uncanny desire was more than satisfied. Surely this is a very sinister side of existence—of the privilege of consciousness itself, and the first thought which brought on these delineations is the Lie of the sneaking sycophant, the Druj, She-Devil, first daughter of the king Dushahu.

Then comes, less sickening, but still revolting, the Akem Manah. It, or "he," stands out as against Vohumanah; as the Druj stands out against Asha; and we may well term it Hate, the concentration of woe's passions, as the Druj was their inception—the continued forth-actkm of the doomed nature. As the mother in the love of Vohu Manah yearns after her little second self, her transmitted soul, so the Akem Manah, blind Fury of Aeshma, stands ready to destroy it. Fair youths, each moved with noblest instincts, still meet in murderous conflict, and fathers mourn their life's lost hopes;—for what? Wars hated by mothers still wrap whole continents in flames, as blight wipes away wide provinces of ripening food. Famine falls upon the world's most simple living inhabitants.

Pestilence strikes terror where it does not more mercifully, swiftly kill—while frightful nightmares of futurity cloud the early days of the thoughtful child, diverting at times even the strong man's life to worthless channels later on, and the dying sometimes await with benumbed conviction the frights of certain Hell, merciful Nature deadening the otherwise tortured faculties. It is the Akem Manah, "the Evil plan" as we might almost term it, preferring also perhaps the other form of the adjective, the superlative ***achishtem*** ; — not the "evil" only but the ***"Worst"*** Mind;— and this, always according to the analogies worked out through implication, is what murderously conflicted with our Vohu Manah everywhere—poisoning the thoughts of that blessed instinct of "Good-Will." And as against God's Authority Khshathra, benignant and merciful, restraining only to compact, ameliorate and save, we have the overwhelming despots of Dush Khshathra. Government, meant to be the arm of truth and God's right hand, and raised aloft for good to repress the outbursting impulses of the young, to protect the wronged,—and punish the agents of the Akem Manah, is met by the Evil Power. At times, even affected with uncontrolled cerebral mania,—the half mad imbeciles of despotism, that is of "inverted power," wreak vengeance on the innocent for their existence and their excellence, taking from their children's lips the bread of sustenance. Those who save their country by great deeds must be prepared for simple murder. Hard earned results stored carefully for an evil day are snatched off in a moment;— slaves must see their labor's wage paid to their masters, with gross indulgence for their recompense. Justice must be laughed at and the silliest of untruths laboriously propagated.

Or, again, wild chaos must sweep everything in the poor hopeless efforts at reform,—too much force being less fatal than too little. Tyranny in the form of

Anarchy leaves misery redoubled. The helpless blinded lead on the poorer blind. Indiscipline, false liberty, leaves all things lost.—Such was the Dush-Khshathra, essence of the impulses which lived in the tyrants of the Yasna.

And then for Aramaiti, God's self-moved inspiration in the good, there was Taramaiti,—the Insolence Irre-pressible, bold genius of effrontery. It was by implication and from analogies active like the Aramaiti, and it gloried in its shame. It was what makes a mock of piety shouting its wild chorus in ribald chants to infamy; it was the wantonness of the Lie, the Hate, the Tyranny, while bla-tant.

We know such things too plainly—they are the shrieks from our madhouse windows, the travestied hymns of midnight streets, the crime of those who "draw iniquity with a cord of vanity, and sin as it were with a cart rope." And there is then its fell result—the very **Completeness,** Haurvatat, of the Holy God has, on this doctrine, its awful negative. The Supreme (?) Deity faces a territory which He Himself has never trod, while His adversary has his emissaries everywhere within His own dominions —with the result that all is approximately marred. Disease, to state the first cursed evil now suggested here, stands ready in a thousand forms to terrify as well as ruin. That one firm work of God, the blest balance of the bodily and mental powers which we call Health, sole condition of effective normal action, is jeoparded.

Demoniac laughter greets foul evils worse than leprosy; poisons which revolt the touch and nostril are lightly passed along; the dying agonies of helpless hearts are made the call for roars of approbation, while to the good, a sorrow well-nigh intensified to mania at times settles over everything; the wine cup with its lighter ruin has given place to the scorching flame of the spirit poison put to the lips of the helpless poor, while the cyclone of financial panic sweeps over the face of populations white with terror, like the face of Ocean swept white with hurricanes, wrecking homes forever;—the treason of some thieving fiend fills up the cup, turning the household to the streets, capped by the remorse of the silly victim, trusting the man hyena with his all.

Haurvatat, the blessed Real of the Ideal, is indeed met by an Incompleteness which has made us almost doubt whether the Evil One of the Two Colossi has not indeed sometimes had the upper hand; and whether life itself be not the curse of all of us.

And as against the Immortal Being of our God the Life-Spirit-Lord, and that of His saints in Earth and Heaven there was, and is, the ever dread alternative;—as seen above.

Even where we are awake to see in Her, nature's soft second nurse, the sweet ending of a life well spent, a fight well fought,—yet, how we recoil—poor self-blinded human nature that we are—aye, how we recoil even from that calm non-entity from which we came. Then what Death is not to the Dying it is that redoubled to the bereaved: to miss the beloved form; to see the dear face fade away— here agonies are real indeed; and the end though it be not indeed the King of terrors, yet it is verily the Queen of sorrows,—*indomitaeque morti!*

Such are the Six Attributes of the Antagonistic Being —extracted by ourselves from the course of Gathic thought.—The deeper Searcher, let me say it here in passing,—who is more anxiously scrutinizing the interior psychic forces here present, will be gratified to see our one main point here strengthened. These Attributes—let us note it well in passing—are still only one of them at all with certainty *personified* ; and, as said above, they are nowhere gathered like the Holy Seven; and this points that most incisive of phenomena, the strange deep abstract nature of the Six, for if five of the six corresponding qualities of Angra Mainyu gathered by ourselves from the antitheses of the Gatha are thus so obviously abstract, this strong fact goes to make out the abstractness of our collected six beatifications all the more distinctly; and it is on this that momentous issues of the past once hung. Yet the two chief ones of each of the Seven, I mean Ahura and Angra Mainyu—are here personified beyond all manner of doubt, God as Ahura Mazda, with His fell opponent. It might be considered strange indeed that I should for one moment mention such a thing so obvious; but here I must be thorough and exhaustive in a certain light of it. Some of my readers will doubtless understand why I dwell on such an apparently all-obvious item. They are indeed great conscious beings personified, and beyond all doubt of it the first ever so presented in all history; and we should pause here to recall and gather up all that this great fact has in it.

The Codes Of Hammurabi And Moses
W. W. Davies

QTY

The discovery of the Hammurabi Code is one of the greatest achievements of archaeology, and is of paramount interest, not only to the student of the Bible, but also to all those interested in ancient history...

Religion   **ISBN:** *1-59462-338-4*   **Pages:132**
MSRP $12.95

The Theory of Moral Sentiments
Adam Smith

QTY

This work from 1749. contains original theories of conscience amd moral judgment and it is the foundation for systemof morals.

Philosophy   **ISBN:** *1-59462-777-0*   **Pages:536**
MSRP $19.95

Jessica's First Prayer
Hesba Stretton

QTY

In a screened and secluded corner of one of the many railway-bridges which span the streets of London there could be seen a few years ago, from five o'clock every morning until half past eight, a tidily set-out coffee-stall, consisting of a trestle and board, upon which stood two large tin cans, with a small fire of charcoal burning under each so as to keep the coffee boiling during the early hours of the morning when the work-people were thronging into the city on their way to their daily toil...

Childrens   **ISBN:** *1-59462-373-2*   **Pages:84**
MSRP $9.95

My Life and Work
Henry Ford

QTY

Henry Ford revolutionized the world with his implementation of mass production for the Model T automobile. Gain valuable business insight into his life and work with his own auto-biography... "We have only started on our development of our country we have not as yet, with all our talk of wonderful progress, done more than scratch the surface. The progress has been wonderful enough but..."

Biographies/   **ISBN:** *1-59462-198-5*   **Pages:300**
MSRP $21.95

The Art of Cross-Examination
Francis Wellman

QTY

I presume it is the experience of every author, after his first book is published upon an important subject, to be almost overwhelmed with a wealth of ideas and illustrations which could readily have been included in his book, and which to his own mind, at least, seem to make a second edition inevitable. Such certainly was the case with me; and when the first edition had reached its sixth impression in five months, I rejoiced to learn that it seemed to my publishers that the book had met with a sufficiently favorable reception to justify a second and considerably enlarged edition. ..

Pages:412

Reference   **ISBN: *1-59462-647-2***   *MSRP $19.95*

On the Duty of Civil Disobedience
Henry David Thoreau

QTY

Thoreau wrote his famous essay, On the Duty of Civil Disobedience, as a protest against an unjust but popular war and the immoral but popular institution of slave-owning. He did more than write—he declined to pay his taxes, and was hauled off to gaol in consequence. Who can say how much this refusal of his hastened the end of the war and of slavery ?

Law   **ISBN: *1-59462-747-9***   **Pages:48**

MSRP $7.45

Dream Psychology
Psychoanalysis for Beginners

Sigmund Freud

Dream Psychology Psychoanalysis for Beginners
Sigmund Freud

QTY

Sigmund Freud, born Sigismund Schlomo Freud (May 6, 1856 - September 23, 1939), was a Jewish-Austrian neurologist and psychiatrist who co-founded the psychoanalytic school of psychology. Freud is best known for his theories of the unconscious mind, especially involving the mechanism of repression; his redefinition of sexual desire as mobile and directed towards a wide variety of objects; and his therapeutic techniques, especially his understanding of transference in the therapeutic relationship and the presumed value of dreams as sources of insight into unconscious desires.

Pages:196

Psychology   **ISBN: *1-59462-905-6***   *MSRP $15.45*

The Miracle of Right Thought
Orison Swett Marden

QTY

Believe with all of your heart that you will do what you were made to do. When the mind has once formed the habit of holding cheerful, happy, prosperous pictures, it will not be easy to form the opposite habit. It does not matter how improbable or how far away this realization may see, or how dark the prospects may be, if we visualize them as best we can, as vividly as possible, hold tenaciously to them and vigorously struggle to attain them, they will gradually become actualized, realized in the life. But a desire, a longing without endeavor, a yearning abandoned or held indifferently will vanish without realization.

Pages:360

Self Help   **ISBN: *1-59462-644-8***   *MSRP $25.45*

QTY

The Rosicrucian Cosmo-Conception Mystic Christianity *by Max Heindel*   ISBN: *1-59462-188-8*   **$38.95**
The Rosicrucian Cosmo-conception is not dogmatic, neither does it appeal to any other authority than the reason of the student. It is: not controversial, but is: sent forth in the, hope that it may help to clear...   New Age/Religion Pages 646

Abandonment To Divine Providence *by Jean-Pierre de Caussade*   ISBN: *1-59462-228-0*   **$25.95**
"The Rev. Jean Pierre de Caussade was one of the most remarkable spiritual writers of the Society of Jesus in France in the 18th Century. His death took place at Toulouse in 1751. His works have gone through many editions and have been republished...   Inspirational/Religion Pages 400

Mental Chemistry *by Charles Haanel*   ISBN: *1-59462-192-6*   **$23.95**
Mental Chemistry allows the change of material conditions by combining and appropriately utilizing the power of the mind. Much like applied chemistry creates something new and unique out of careful combinations of chemicals the mastery of mental chemistry...   New Age Pages 354

The Letters of Robert Browning and Elizabeth Barret Barrett 1845-1846 vol II   ISBN: *1-59462-193-4*   **$35.95**
by Robert Browning and Elizabeth Barrett
Biographies Pages 596

Gleanings In Genesis (volume I) *by Arthur W. Pink*   ISBN: *1-59462-130-6*   **$27.45**
Appropriately has Genesis been termed "the seed plot of the Bible" for in it we have, in germ form, almost all of the great doctrines which are afterwards fully developed in the books of Scripture which follow...   Religion/Inspirational Pages 420

The Master Key *by L. W. de Laurence*   ISBN: *1-59462-001-6*   **$30.95**
In no branch of human knowledge has there been a more lively increase of the spirit of research during the past few years than in the study of Psychology, Concentration and Mental Discipline. The requests for authentic lessons in Thought Control, Mental Discipline and...   New Age/Business Pages 422

The Lesser Key Of Solomon Goetia *by L. W. de Laurence*   ISBN: *1-59462-092-X*   **$9.95**
This translation of the first book of the "Lernegton" which is now for the first time made accessible to students of Talismanic Magic was done, after careful collation and edition, from numerous Ancient Manuscripts in Hebrew, Latin, and French...   New Age/Occult Pages 92

Rubaiyat Of Omar Khayyam *by Edward Fitzgerald*   ISBN:*1-59462-332-5*   **$13.95**
Edward Fitzgerald, whom the world has already learned, in spite of his own efforts to remain within the shadow of anonymity, to look upon as one of the rarest poets of the century, was born at Bredfield, in Suffolk, on the 31st of March, 1809. He was the third son of John Purcell...   Music Pages 172

Ancient Law *by Henry Maine*   ISBN: *1-59462-128-4*   **$29.95**
The chief object of the following pages is to indicate some of the earliest ideas of mankind, as they are reflected in Ancient Law, and to point out the relation of those ideas to modern thought.   Religiom/History Pages 452

Far-Away Stories *by William J. Locke*   ISBN: *1-59462-129-2*   **$19.45**
"Good wine needs no bush, but a collection of mixed vintages does. And this book is just such a collection. Some of the stories I do not want to remain buried for ever in the museum files of dead magazine-numbers an author's not unpardonable vanity..."   Fiction Pages 272

Life of David Crockett *by David Crockett*   ISBN: *1-59462-250-7*   **$27.45**
"Colonel David Crockett was one of the most remarkable men of the times in which he lived. Born in humble life, but gifted with a strong will, an indomitable courage, and unremitting perseverance...   Biographies/New Age Pages 424

Lip-Reading *by Edward Nitchie*   ISBN: *1-59462-206-X*   **$25.95**
Edward B. Nitchie, founder of the New York School for the Hard of Hearing, now the Nitchie School of Lip-Reading, Inc, wrote "LIP-READING Principles and Practice". The development and perfecting of this meritorious work on lip-reading was an undertaking...   How-to Pages 400

A Handbook of Suggestive Therapeutics, Applied Hypnotism, Psychic Science   ISBN: *1-59462-214-0*   **$24.95**
by Henry Munro
Health/New Age/Health/Self-help Pages 376

A Doll's House: and Two Other Plays *by Henrik Ibsen*   ISBN: *1-59462-112-8*   **$19.95**
Henrik Ibsen created this classic when in revolutionary 1848 Rome. Introducing some striking concepts in playwriting for the realist genre, this play has been studied the world over.   Fiction/Classics/Plays 308

The Light of Asia *by sir Edwin Arnold*   ISBN: *1-59462-204-3*   **$13.95**
In this poetic masterpiece, Edwin Arnold describes the life and teachings of Buddha. The man who was to become known as Buddha to the world was born as Prince Gautama of India but he rejected the worldly riches and abandoned the reigns of power when...   Religion/History/Biographies Pages 170

The Complete Works of Guy de Maupassant *by Guy de Maupassant*   ISBN: *1-59462-157-8*   **$16.95**
"For days and days, nights and nights, I had dreamed of that first kiss which was to consecrate our engagement, and I knew not on what spot I should put my lips..."   Fiction/Classics Pages 240

The Art of Cross-Examination *by Francis L. Wellman*   ISBN: *1-59462-309-0*   **$26.95**
Written by a renowned trial lawyer, Wellman imparts his experience and uses case studies to explain how to use psychology to extract desired information through questioning.   How-to/Science/Reference Pages 408

Answered or Unanswered? *by Louisa Vaughan*   ISBN: *1-59462-248-5*   **$10.95**
Miracles of Faith in China
Religion Pages 112

The Edinburgh Lectures on Mental Science (1909) *by Thomas*   ISBN: *1-59462-008-3*   **$11.95**
This book contains the substance of a course of lectures recently given by the writer in the Queen Street Hail, Edinburgh. Its purpose is to indicate the Natural Principles governing the relation between Mental Action and Material Conditions...   New Age/Psychology Pages 148

Ayesha *by H. Rider Haggard*   ISBN: *1-59462-301-5*   **$24.95**
Verily and indeed it is the unexpected that happens! Probably if there was one person upon the earth from whom the Editor of this, and of a certain previous history, did not expect to hear again...   Classics Pages 380

Ayala's Angel *by Anthony Trollope*   ISBN: *1-59462-352-X*   **$29.95**
The two girls were both pretty, but Lucy who was twenty-one who supposed to be simple and comparatively unattractive, whereas Ayala was credited, as her Bombwhat romantic name might show, with poetic charm and a taste for romance. Ayala when her father died was nineteen...   Fiction Pages 484

The American Commonwealth *by James Bryce*   ISBN: *1-59462-286-8*   **$34.45**
An interpretation of American democratic political theory. It examines political mechanics and society from the perspective of Scotsman James Bryce   Politics Pages 572

Stories of the Pilgrims *by Margaret P. Pumphrey*   ISBN: *1-59462-116-0*   **$17.95**
This book explores pilgrims religious oppression in England as well as their escape to Holland and eventual crossing to America on the Mayflower, and their early days in New England...   History Pages 268

www.bookjungle.com *email: sales@bookjungle.com fax: 630-214-0564 mail: Book Jungle PO Box 2226 Champaign, IL 61825*

QTY

The Fasting Cure *by Sinclair Upton* ISBN: *1-59462-222-1* **$13.95**
In the Cosmopolitan Magazine for May, 1910, and in the Contemporary Review (London) for April, 1910, I published an article dealing with my experiences in fasting. I have written a great many magazine articles, but never one which attracted so much attention... New Age/Self Help/Health Pages 164

Hebrew Astrology *by Sepharial* ISBN: *1-59462-308-2* **$13.45**
In these days of advanced thinking it is a matter of common observation that we have left many of the old landmarks behind and that we are now pressing forward to greater heights and to a wider horizon than that which represented the mind-content of our progenitors... Astrology Pages 144

Thought Vibration or The Law of Attraction in the Thought World ISBN: *1-59462-127-6* **$12.95**
by William Walker Atkinson *Psychology/Religion Pages 144*

Optimism *by Helen Keller* ISBN: *1-59462-108-X* **$15.95**
Helen Keller was blind, deaf, and mute since 19 months old, yet famously learned how to overcome these handicaps, communicate with the world, and spread her lectures promoting optimism. An inspiring read for everyone... Biographies/Inspirational Pages 84

Sara Crewe *by Frances Burnett* ISBN: *1-59462-360-0* **$9.45**
In the first place, Miss Minchin lived in London. Her home was a large, dull, tall one, in a large, dull square, where all the houses were alike, and all the sparrows were alike, and where all the door-knockers made the same heavy sound... Childrens/Classic Pages 88

The Autobiography of Benjamin Franklin *by Benjamin Franklin* ISBN: *1-59462-135-7* **$24.95**
The Autobiography of Benjamin Franklin has probably been more extensively read than any other American historical work, and no other book of its kind has had such ups and downs of fortune. Franklin lived for many years in England, where he was agent... Biographies/History Pages 332

Name	
Email	
Telephone	
Address	
City, State ZIP	

☐ Credit Card   ☐ Check / Money Order

Credit Card Number	
Expiration Date	
Signature	

Please Mail to: Book Jungle
PO Box 2226
Champaign, IL 61825
or Fax to: 630-214-0564

ORDERING INFORMATION
web: *www.bookjungle.com*
email: *sales@bookjungle.com*
fax: *630-214-0564*
mail: *Book Jungle PO Box 2226 Champaign, IL 61825*
or PayPal *to sales@bookjungle.com*

Please contact us for bulk discounts

DIRECT-ORDER TERMS

20% Discount if You Order Two or More Books
Free Domestic Shipping!
Accepted: Master Card, Visa, Discover, American Express

www.ingramcontent.com/pod-product-compliance
Lightning Source LLC
Chambersburg PA
CBHW081158170626

46813CB00009B/3242